Diary of a Triflin' Bitch

By:

Platinum

Diary of a Triflin' Bitch

Diary of a Triflin' Bitch

Copyright © 2014 by Bridget Jones. All rights reserved. No part of this publication may be reproduced, distributed, or transmitted in any form or by any means, including photocopying, recording, or other electronic or mechanical methods, without the prior written permission of the publisher, Right Circle Publications, except in the case of brief quotations embodied in critical reviews and certain other noncommercial uses permitted by copyright law. For permission requests contact the publisher.

Dedication

To my mother Ms. Loretta Jones thanks for raising me to be the strong, black, independent woman I am today. My kids, Marquez, Breshawna, Aniya, Xyir and Tracy you all are the reason I go hard in this game. To my grandmother Prealie and my poppa Amos thanks for being my back bone. I love you guys.

Acknowledgements

This is totally a dream come true for me and for that I praise him. I give honor to GOD for allowing me the opportunity to be put in this position. I thank you Father for the many blessings you send down upon me and my family. To my sisters Tiffany, Jessica and Yolonda thank you all for being there for me when the world let me down. To my best friend Ronita thanks for the love you give me every day. To my father William thanks for being who you are. To my brothers Michael, William Jr and Jeremy I love you all. To a special friend Terrance thanks for giving me my first urban street fiction book to read, I love you brother. To my kids Marquez, Breshawna, Aniya, Xyir and my godson Tracy I thank the lord for bringing all of you in my life. You guys are the reason I go hard in everything I do. All of you never give up in life, you all can be and do anything you want to do. I love you guys with all of my heart. Without you there will be no me.

To Jermaine, thanks cousin for being that one person who never doubted any and everything that I do. Thanks for being there for me day and night. You are my

Diary of a Triflin' Bitch

favoritest cousin in the whole wide world. I love you to pieces boo. Thanks for being who you are.

To my extended family over at Right Circle Publications Lisa Wells, Jennifer Brooks, Aishah Flood, and David Weaver thanks for giving me a chance at a new life. Thanks for the many talks and the words of encouragement. #TBRS for life! It feels good to have found a home and thanks for welcoming me with open arms. For that alone I have much love for each and every one of you.

Thanks to my editors for working with me on this book. Thanks for the new ideas and or the many changes we had to make. Love you also.

Special thanks to my readers and all the bookstores who agreed to support me. Thanks in advance for the support going forward.

I do apologize in advance if I have forgotten anybody. I want to thank you now. You know who you are and what you mean to me. Thanks again to my readers and supporters. Your feedback is inspiring to me.

July 2013

Brandy

"OMG I'm about to cum". Brandy yelled as sweat poured down her forehead. Jay was giving her the ride of her life outside, behind the house. Brandy and Jay knew they were wrong for what they were doing, but their adrenaline was running on high and neither one of them cared at that moment. Jay continued to hit the right spot as he tried to quiet Brandy down by putting his hand over her mouth. There was a party going on inside the house for another one of their home-girls and he didn't want them to get caught. Diamond, his steady girl of five years was inside the house also. Jay pumped one last time then he dropped to his knees and attacked Brandy's clit with hunger. He knew when he did this to Diamond she was always speechless, so he had to try something to get Brandy to quiet down. He felt she was being loud on purpose, and he hated a messy bitch.

Diary of a Triflin' Bitch

Brandy threw her head back and rode Jay's face until she was hit with a mind blowing orgasm. Her voice was gone, and she couldn't make a sound as her legs shook, she unloaded a bucket of cum down Jay's throat. Jay had a rule about eating pussy, but he had two things he needed Brandy to do for him so he had to make this quickie a good one. He hated her, and she was about to find out just how much.

As the orgasm stopped, Jay stood up and wiped his mouth with the back of his hand while pulling the rubber off. He instructed Brandy to finish him off as well. Brandy hated when he did that; she wanted him to cum inside of her, but she think he had caught on to her little game. She loved the sex, but the thought of putting his dick in her mouth after it has been all up in her bestie was nasty and discussing. Jay forced Brandy to her knees and face fucked her until he felt his nut about to come up, he pulled out of her mouth and came all over her face. Brandy was pissed, but she knew she better not say one word-out the way to Jay. He was a nice guy, but had a bad side that she didn't want to get on. Jay considers himself a good dude but felt guilty about what he was doing with his girl's best friend.

Diary of a Triflin' Bitch

As Jay zipped up his pants and started to walk away from Brandy, he yelled over his shoulder at her "Hit me later I got some business for you to take care of." With that he was gone; he had to go brush his teeth before he go back in the house. His home boy stayed three doors down so it wouldn't take him long to get back. Brandy, on the other hand, was tired of Jay fucking and leaving her. She wanted him for herself, but didn't know how to tell him. They had been fucking each other now for six months. Brandy had to find a way to get back into the party before she was missed, however, she had to get Jay's cum off her face. She ran to her car and dug around in the trunk until she found some of her panties she had worn a week ago. Brandy pretty much lived out of her car; she refused to go back home to her parent's house and endure the hell she went through. Brandy wiped cum off her face then closed her trunk only to be face to face with Diamond. "Shit girl you scared me, were you came from?" Was the only thing Brandy could think about at that moment to say, she just knew she was caught.

"I was looking for Jay, have you seen him? He's not in the house I checked, and one of his boys is looking for

Diary of a Triflin' Bitch

him." Diamond felt like Brandy was up to something but she just couldn't put her finger on it. Brandy and Jay had both been MIA for about forty-five minutes and she had a feeling they were together.

"Oh girl he ran up the street, he said he had a sell to go make at Dayshawn house. He told me to tell you he will be right back." Said Brandy

"So what are you doing out here all by yourself?" Diamond wanted to see were her head was at. Something was strange bout Brandy and Diamond wanted to get to the bottom of it.

"Umm I just got out the car with my boo thang. Girl you know how I do when it's time to get this money." Brandy hands started to sweat because she felt pressured.

"Your ass is nasty, so what you wasn't gonna bathe your ass after fucking some nigga. Bitch I see why your ass don't have no man!" Diamond couldn't do nothing but shake her head. She knew her friend was thirsty but damn!

Diary of a Triflin' Bitch

"Nawl girl I was just about to come tell you that I was finna go to your house to wash up, I need your house keys." Brandy was ready to go because her friend was making her nervous. She really didn't care for her friends feelings she just didn't want her to find out about her little secret just yet. She was trying to get pregnant by Jay first, that way he couldn't leave her. He would be stuck with her for the next 18 years and she would be straight.

"Ok girl Tip is waiting on all of us so she can cut her cake, so hurry up and get back." Diamond said handing Brandy her house key and then walked away to go call Jay ass.

Chapter 1

Best friends

In the Beginning (August 2008)

In the hood is where the girls met. Tiponya aka Tip and Brandy are sisters. Brandy's best friend was Diamond, and Tracy was Tip and Brandy's cousin. When you saw one the other three weren't too far behind. Tip was the oldest of them all. Tip was a bad bitch at the age of seventeen. She was 5'5, and 140 pounds, double D breast and hips to die for. Tip made sure she stayed dress, that's why she was the most hated in her high school. Tip had a boyfriend that sold a little weed and made sure he laced his girl as much as he could. But what he didn't know was he wasn't the only man to give money to Tip. Tip was still a virgin down bottom but her mouth had miles on it.

Brandy was fifteen years old, 5'7", and weighed 160 pounds, light skinned with long jet black hair down her back. She wanted to be just like her sister but had the game

Diary of a Triflin' Bitch

all messed up. Brandy was a mutt, as the boys in their neighborhood called her. Brandy learned at an early age to try to suck and fuck her way to the top. She had been fucked in every hole on her body. Brandy lost her virginity at the early age of twelve. Her parents had to put her on birth control so she wouldn't get pregnant and become a teenage mother.

Diamond was the same age as Brandy, but she was the total opposite as her. She was the color of caramel, had burgundy highlights, long eye lashes, and she was 5'9, 130 pounds, and an ass that would make a grown man cry. Diamond was a lady at all cost; when she went to school she dress classy, she always wore heels. Diamond lived with her aunt, because her mother had died from an over dose of crack cocaine and her dad was the man who sold it to her. She hated her daddy with a passion. She never wanted to see his face.

Tracy was sixteen years old and was the quiet type, she hated drama. She was dark chocolate, 5'10, 166 pounds, and had short hair. Tracy made straight A's in school and didn't have time for boys. She was a virgin and was

Diary of a Triflin' Bitch

planning on waiting until she got married to lose her virginity. She had one boy she was interested in, but not enough to lose her virginity.

One day on the way home from school a nice clean canary yellow Dodge Durango pulled up alongside of them. The driver, whose name was Dayshawn, was mesmerized by the four beautiful girls walking down the road. "Damn dawg these chicks are bad as fuck." Dayshawn said. "Man hurry the fuck up we got to go pick up this money." Jay said. They were making pickups on this Good Friday.

"Hey you, in them jean pants damn you bad. What's your name?" Dayshawn said to Tracy. This put a smile on her face. She was real shy when it came down to talking to men. She just stood there staring at him. Brandy was the bold one out of the bunch she spoke up for her. "Hey boo her name is Tracy, what's yours?" Brandy smiled she knew these men were in the big league and she wanted in. Brandy had her eyes on the passenger, but he had his eyes on Diamond.

Diary of a Triflin' Bitch

Dayshawn said "Tracy can I holla at cha for a minute?" Tracy walked up to the truck but got bumped out the way by Brandy. This pissed Tip off cause she knew how her sister got down, and she didn't want Brandy to mess things up for Tracy. But Dayshawn spoke up before Tip could say something.

"Damn lil mama I'm trying to holla at your girl, not you." He was mad over how thirsty this lil bitch was. "Nigga please it ain't that serious, I don't want you anyways, I wanna holla at your boy!" She said eyeing Jay cause she seen she wasn't going to get anywhere with him. "Jay she is all yours!" He laughed at the thought of her not having a chance with his boy. Dayshawn knew what type of female Jay dealt with and she was not it.

"Nawl dawg I'm cool, plus we need to go handle this business." Jay was about to blow a gasket at the thought of being around Brandy. He knew she was young and had a young girls mind but he also had seen one of the girls he wanted, so he had to try his hand. "Aye shawty you over there with the braids, let me holla at you for a minute." Jay smiled at Diamond.

Diary of a Triflin' Bitch

Diamond walked around the truck to go holla at Jay. "What's up boo?" Diamond said as she stepped close to the truck. Jay and Diamond talk for about ten minutes and then they exchanged numbers promising to keep in touch. At the end of their conversation, both of them wore a smile.

Seeing her girl get her mack on, Tracy loosened up a little and started to talk to Dayshawn. They finished their conversation with Tracy getting Dayshawn's number because she couldn't have boys calling her house.

"Alright ladies we will holla at y'all later, y'all be easy." Dayshawn said to the girls as he was pulling away from the curb.

As the men pulled away from the girls, Tip went ham on Brandy, "Really hoe you almost fucked that up for my girl over here!" She said pointing at Tracy. Brandy was pissed she didn't get one of the men in the truck. She really was attracted to Jay but he had chosen Diamond and that pissed her off to the max. Right then and there she was very envious of Diamond and wanted everything she had.

Diary of a Triflin' Bitch

"Whatever hoe she wasn't trying to speak up, so I went for it, hell I know money when I see it." She rolled her eyes at her sister.

"Well first of all I don't need no one to speak up for me, and second of all hoe I can speak for myself!" yelled Tracy. She was feeling some type of way about the way Brandy was acting. She hated when she acted that way. Everybody was quite because Tracy was the laid back one of the group, and she rarely cussed. All of them knew not to mess with her. Brandy on the other hand, felt froggy so she came back at Tracy, "Hoe you was standing there all mute and shit like you was deaf!" Before Brandy couldn't say another word she was hit in the mouth by Tracy, it happened so fast Tracy was on her ass like white on rice. It took three of the girls to pull Tracy off Brandy. Tracy was feed up with Brandy's mouth, so she decided to shut her up. This is how their bitter sweet relationship started. From that point on Brandy had it out for all three of their asses. She hated Tracy because she knew she couldn't beat her, she hated her sister because she always felt she took up for Diamond and Tracy, and she hated Diamond because she felt like Diamond took what was supposed to be hers. JAY!

Chapter 2

The Crew

(June 2012)

    The house was dark when Brandy rolled over; she had just completed the first part of her plan. Now the second part was unlock the back door so Tee Tee and Anthony could get into the house. Ant was one of her many boo's but was her main man. Brandy crept out the bed with Kash and headed for the bathroom. When she got in the bathroom, she sat on the toilet to release the pressure from her night of passion she just had. Kash was a made man with a lot of dough. Brandy had been lurking and trying to snag him for a minute. Brandy finished in the bathroom washed her hands and turned out the lights. She was trying to make her way out the room when Kash turned over and sat straight up in the bed, "Where the hell are you going?" He asked while pointing his 45 at her in the dark. He never trusted anyone so when she got out the bed he instantly

Diary of a Triflin' Bitch

woke up. Brandy was unawlare of the gun being pointed at her.

"Oh bae I was going to the kitchen to get something to drink, you wore me out earlier. Do you want anything while I'm there?" She asked nervously smiling.

"Nawl I'm good, hurry back daddy got something he want to give you." he said trying to put his gun under his pillow were he kept it.

Brandy almost threw up at the thought of fucking Kash again. Kash wasn't a very good looker and his dick was small as a pencil, but his money was what she wanted. She would do whatever it takes to get what she wanted. As she made her way to the back door, she stopped at the refrigerator to grab a soda to wash down the bad taste she had in her mouth. Brandy unlocked the door and in stepped Tee Tee and Ant, "Hoe what took you so long, was that dick that good." Ant asked pissed at the thought of another man's hand on his woman. But this is how he made most of his money. "Damn it Ant let me do my thang, I had to put the nigga to sleep with this good good first. And keep your

Diary of a Triflin' Bitch

voice down he awake now, I got to go. Give me about thirty minutes to an hour." With that being said, she grabbed her soda and headed back to the room where Kash was. Ant wanted to dome her and Kash's ass at that moment, but his heart wouldn't let him do it because he had fell in love with Brandy the first time he saw her.

Meanwhile, Kash had Brandy bend over the bed trying his best to dig her back out. She was playing her part making noises moaning and groaning to stroke his ego. "Oh big daddy get this pussy!" she yells as quite as she can, she didn't want Ant to hear her. It was too late, he heard the bed rocking first as he eased up the hallway. As he got closer, he heard Brandy's moans and started to see red. Tee Tee had to hold him back because he knew his cousin was about to go off. Tee Tee pushed the bedroom door open slightly and aimed his gun in the direction were Brandy's moans was coming from. It was so dark in the room he couldn't get a good aim on his target. Ant stepped in the room after Tee Tee and hit the lights, "Don't move asshole!" Tee Tee said now with his gun pointed at Kash's head. Kash was so caught off guard that he had to give

Diary of a Triflin' Bitch

Brandy's pussy one more pump. This pissed Ant off to the max; he fired a warning shot at him.

"Pussy nigga get your dick out of my old lady." Kash's face turned completely red at that statement. He felt the betrayal of being set up. He eased his now limp dick out of Brandy, and she ran to the other side of the bed to get her clothes to get dress. "Man what the hell is this all about, I hope not your chick because she came on to me. I got cash and can pay you, how much you want man?" Kash stated he was trying to figure out a way to get to his gun. "Nawl homie it's not about my chick, but we gonna take your money! Now where is it?" Ant said. Kash knew if he didn't give up the cash he was gonna die. So he lunged towards the pillow where his gun was, but didn't have a chance as soon as he moved a bullet from Brandy's gun went straight through his eyes. Before Kash's body hit the bed, he was dead.

"Why the hell you do that?" Tee Tee yelled. He wanted to press Kash a lil more about where the money was.

Diary of a Triflin' Bitch

"Look!" Brandy said as she lifted up the pillow to show them what Kash was going for. "This is where he kept his gun at all times."

"We still needed to know where he kept his money at!" Ant screamed. He was still feeling some type of way about her fucking this nigga.

"His safe is in the basement and the code to the safe is 39 right, 42 left, and 3 right. We got to move quickly because you didn't use the silencer so I know his neighbors heard the gun shot." Ant and Tee Tee took off running towards the basement, but Brandy's sneaky ass stayed behind because she knew he had another safe in the bedroom closet. She wanted that cash all to herself. Brandy ran to the safe in the closet to retrieve the cash and its contents. The safe was already open, so it made her take quick and easy. Brandy stuffed the cash in her purse and then took off down the hallway. When she got to the basement Ant and Tee Tee were just finishing up with putting the cash in their gym bags. There take looked to be over a hundred grand, and the men were satisfied with that.

Diary of a Triflin' Bitch

"Okay, we been here to long, man let's go." Tee Tee said as he heard the sirens in the distance. The trio took off running out the back door towards the car that was parked seven houses down the road. As they piled into the car, they saw the first police car pull on the street. They all ducked down to go unnoticed. The police cars circled the block until a nosey white guy pointed him in the direction of the house were the gun shot came from. As the cop made his way to the front door to scope out the crime scene, Ant pulled out of the driveway and fled. The ride back to the city was quiet and seemed long. They were about an hour away from home so Ant had to keep cool and drive the speed limit. Tee Tee turned on the CD player in the car and music started to pour out of the speakers. He knew as soon as they made it to the safe house Ant and Brandy were gonna start the bullshit. It always happened after every lick. He was ready to count up this money and leave them. He just didn't understand why Ant kept fucking with Brandy. Everybody in the hood knew she was a mutt. He even had his way with her for $20 and some coke. He got the bitch high, had his way with her and then gave her ass $20 dollars and sent her ass on her merry way.

Chapter 3

Safe House

The safe house was a house that Tee Tee was renting, nobody knew about this spot but the three of them. It was an old house on the outside, but the inside was decked out. It had 3 bedrooms, 2 ½ bathrooms, a black leather sectional sat in one corner, a 60 inch flat screen TV mounted on the wall and a mini bar in the other corner. One bedroom was the safe room. This is where they went to count all the money from their licks. It had three safes in the room, one for each of them. The other two rooms were used as guest bedrooms in case it got too late and they didn't want to drive home.

As the trio got into the house Brandy made her way to the bathroom, and the men went straight to the safe room to start counting the money. Tee Tee had a bad bitch that could suck a mean dick he was trying to get her. Brandy closed the door and locked it when she got in the bathroom. She sat on the toilet to count the money she had taken from

Diary of a Triflin' Bitch

the other safe. After counting her dough it came up to 12,792 dollars. This put a smile on her face. Money always made her pussy wet. She couldn't wait to add this to her take from the other safe. Brandy made her way to the safe room, "How much so far?" she asked like nothing was wrong. The money counter was going and was up to 597,789 dollars. Shit was looking real good to all of them.

"We looking great for tonight's take, what took you so long in the bathroom?" Ant asked looking at her. The money counter buzzed signaling that it was done. Tee Tee added another stack of money to the counter. He had three more stacks left to be counted. After about ten more minutes they had their final number from there take. 729,735 dollars, after dividing it three ways everybody got 243,245 dollars. That plus her take from the other safe Brandy had the total of 256,037 dollars.

"Hey now hey, cash is what it is!" yelled Brandy. She was happy with her take but she had to give them the low down on this other dude she had been talking to. Tee Tee was already heading to his safe to put his money up, he already had $200,000 safe. He basically lived off the

Diary of a Triflin' Bitch

money he made from hustling. Ant kept a couple of stacks so he could go splurge a lil for the night, and Brandy put all the money in the safe except for what was in her purse.

Chapter 4

The Meet

All the girls were hanging out today, they hadn't done this in a while. First lunch at Joe's Crab Shack, this is what they did when they had gossip to tell one another, they all took the vow to never talk over the phone because of the business there men were in. As the girls were ordering their food Tip excused herself to go to the bathroom, she wasn't feeling too good she was eight weeks pregnant and was about to spill the beans to her girls. She was already engaged to be married; her life was good.

Tracy started the conversation first, "Okay since we all are here I'm going to go first, me and Dayshawn are over. I'm sick of his cheating ass and all the diseases he keeps bringing me." She got a lot of remarks from her girls it brought tears to her eyes.

"So what are you going to do?" Tip asked. She was the most concerned. She was very heart broken about this

Diary of a Triflin' Bitch

because Tracy had trusted Dayshawn and gave him her virginity, and they had been dating for five plus years. It was very sad to see their relationship come to an end.

"First I got to go to the doctor and see what the hell I got this time, last time it was chlamydia and crabs. His dirty dick ass don't give a fuck about me. But pay back is a bitch." She said as hot tears streamed down her face.

Diamond had to speak up now, "Tracy don't go getting yourself in any trouble, and I'm gonna have a talk with Mr. Jay tonight when he gets his ass home. His boy is out of pocket for this shit!" Diamond was pissed also because she had told Jay to check his boy before. Tracy was a good girl and didn't need that bullshit.

"I'm not gonna get in no trouble and that's why you not gonna say nothing to Jay about this. I want it to be a surprise for his bitch ass. If I got something I can't get rid of I'm gonna kill his punk ass, and that's on my momma." She said just before the waiters came out with their food. The girls waited until the waiters were out of ear shot to respond to Tracy's comment.

Diary of a Triflin' Bitch

"Girl please stop talking like that, he is not worth your freedom. Don't let him knock you off your square like that. But if you are for real about what you just said let me know, I got somebody that can do it for you. He owes me a favor so you won't have to pay nothing." Brandy said trying to conceal her happiness. She was the one who gave Dayshawn chlamydia and trichomoniasis. She was already getting treatment for hers.

"Really Brandy, why would you say something like that to her? We are not even gonna have this conversation because if either of you gets caught, both of you will be in jail for the rest of your lives." Diamond yelled a little louder than she intended to. The girls looked around the restaurant to make sure nobody was paying attention to them.

"Diamond don't worry about it, if anything I will do the deed my damn self. I don't need any witnesses or help." Tracy said.

"Well ladies I have great news for you!" Smiled Tip, she paused until she had everybody attention around the table. When she saw she did she let it roll out of her mouth, "I'm pregnant!" She screamed. Everybody was screaming except Brandy she could care less about any of their happiness.

"Girl is that why your skin is glowing?" Diamond said

"Well I'm only eight weeks, so it's only the beginning. I got a long ways to go. Diamond we want you to be the god mother of our child. Would you grant me and Terry the honor of being the god mother of our first born child?" Tip asked she held her breath waiting for the answer.

"Yes I would love to be the god mother of your child, thanks for thinking of me!" Diamond had tears in her eyes, she felt so loved and blessed to have this opportunity. Tracy noticed Brandy reaction to the news, but she didn't say one word. She knew from that point on she had to watch Brandy's hating ass.

Diary of a Triflin' Bitch

"Well, now that you got me all emotional I might as well tell y'all the dirt." She had to take a few deep breaths to get herself together. "First of all Jay's ass got to go do some time, his lawyer said he has to do a year and a day." She said as another tear rolled down her cheeks. She hated the thought of living one day without him.

"Well, I hope this time you're leaving his ass for good; he is no good for you. I've been telling you that for the last few years." Brandy said. She wanted Diamond to leave Jay while he was in jail so she can be there for him and win him over. Everybody was confused at that remark. It pissed Diamond and Tip off instantly. Diamond was about to say something, but Tracy spoke up first.

"You never have anything good to say to anybody, what the hell is your problem?" Tracy cut her eyes at Brandy. She wanted to jump cross the table and choke the hell out of her.

"This hating ass bitch just jealous cause she don't have a man and no Brandy I'm not gonna leave my man. I'm gonna stand beside him no matter what! As for the

Diary of a Triflin' Bitch

second thing I was gonna tell y'all was that he wants me to take over his spot for him while he is gone."

"See what the hell I'm talking about, a real man wouldn't want his woman out here selling drugs for him, while he goes to do time. He is not a real man!" Brandy yelled.

"I know we all think Brandy be hating, but Diamond think about this for a minute. Do you really think you can take over his spot for a year?" Tip the motherly one of them all asked. She was concerned that something would go wrong and Diamond would get in trouble.

"Yeah Tip, I won't be in the game, I will only have to collect money from one house daily. And he already has it set up for one of his men to pick me up and take me to go do it." Diamond said in a low tone. Meanwhile the whole time she was talking Brandy was scheming on her come up.

"OK if that's all you will be doing I don't see nothing wrong with it, if you don't watch out for your man's money, who will?" Tracy said with a smile.

Diary of a Triflin' Bitch

"But what are you supposed to do with all the money once you collect it?" Tip asked.

"We haven't discussed that as of yet, so right now I really don't know." said Diamond.

"Well friend if you need some help I'm here for you." Brandy said first. She knew she had to keep Diamond close so her plan could come together.

"Me too hun!" Stated Tracy, she would always be down for her girls because they were always down for her.

"Well now that I'm with child Terry won't let me hang to hard, but you can always call me for advice if you need it." Tip said.

"Thanks y'all I really needed that, I'm kind of scared to do it but if I got my girls behind me I will be good." Diamond said. The girls had small talk for the next hour while they ate their food. They all hugged before they departed.

Chapter 5

Brandy

Brandy came on to Jay one night after her girl Diamond went to work. Brandy was a gold digger with a capital G! She was 18-years-old, no kids, and a body to die for. Brandy stood at 5'7", weighed 160, light skin with long jet black hair down her back. She had an ass like an onion. She knew she had a bad body, but always used it for all the wrong reasons. She was staying the night with Diamond because she didn't have anywhere else to go, and tonight none of her boo's wanted to deal with her thirsty ass. She was dealing with five different niggas at the time, and all of them had a lady. Two were married, two were brothers, and one was a nigga she had just met at a stop light. Brandy was just a jump off who wanted to be a hustler's wife. She thought she was playing the game right by sleeping her way to the top. She did everything from fucking, sucking, and setting nigga up to be robbed to get money. Brandy had been doing this for the past two years but she only kept about $500 in cash on her at a time. She wasn't as dumb as

Diary of a Triflin' Bitch

she lead on to be; she had all of her money put up in her safe. None of her girls knew about her money and she planned on keeping it that way. If they all thought she was broke, she was going to keep using them. She also came up with this plan to get pregnant by her best friend's man. Why not? He ran whole city and was getting major money. Brandy knew she had to do something because her money was getting low and she was tired of living from motel to motel.

Brandy was in the guess bedroom watching TV when she heard a car pull into the drive way. She peeped out the curtains and saw Jay stumbling towards the door, and her panties got wet just thinking about him inside of her. She turned off the TV and cracked open the bedroom door.

Jay came home drunk as hell this night. He knew he had to get home before Diamond went to work. He was horny and needed a quickie before his girl went to work. He made his way up the stairs passing the guess bedroom unawlare of Brandy's presence, he went straight to their

Diary of a Triflin' Bitch

bedroom were Diamond was coming out of the bathroom wrapped in a towel dripping wet.

"Damn it Jay, you scared the shit out of me. Why you creeping around in here like that?" Diamond screamed. Jay's dick got hard instantly at the site of Diamond's body. Jay cleared his throat and spoke up, "Sorry bae I just came in and I didn't know you were still here." Jay was lying because Diamond's car was parked in their driveway. Diamond saw Jay's dick get hard, and her hot spot got wet instantly. She knew what was on his mind, and she needed it to. Diamond made her way over to the bed and lay on her back and opened her legs just the way her man liked. Diamond started playing with her perfectly shaved pussy with one hand and called Jay over with the other. Jay didn't waste any time getting to the bed where she was laying. Diamond knew playing with herself turned Jay on in the worse way. When Jay got to the bed, he replaced Diamond's fingers with his tongue. Diamond knew right then and there this was not going to be a quickie because she and her man hadn't had sex in about two weeks.

Diary of a Triflin' Bitch

Jay first flicked his tongue over Diamond's clit; Diamond jumped at the feeling. Jay continued to devour Diamond's love box until he felt her body shiver, he knew she was ready to cum, so he went in for the kill. He sucked her clit into his mouth like a vacuum and applied pressure until she came in his mouth. Diamond's body jerked and shivered for about two minutes straight. She laid there like a limp doll; Jay stood up and admired his handy work. He knew how to put in work when it came down to his woman. Jay climbed on top of Diamond and inserted his nine inches of meat into Diamond's tight walls. Inch by inch Diamond's body came to life, Jay was packing but he knew how to use it. Jay eased his way into her until his whole shaft was deep inside of her. Diamond screamed out in ecstasy from the pain and pleasure her man was giving her. Once Jay's dick was completely wet by Diamond's juices, Jay went to work. Both of them had worked up a sweat. Jay pounded Diamond's back out for thirty minutes straight none stop. He then instructed her to flip over onto her stomach on all fours in the doggie style position. He wanted to hit it from the back. He loved to see Diamond's ass jiggle with his name tatted over her ass "Jamie" which was Jay's real name. Both were so in tuned with each other that they

Diary of a Triflin' Bitch

never saw Brandy standing at the door watching the whole time. Brandy had seen everything and had played with herself until she came twice. Diamond forgot Brandy was staying the night, and Jay never knew she was there, so he didn't close the bedroom door when he came in. Diamond and Jay sexed each other for another ten minutes and Jay finally exploded inside her.

"Why the fuck you did that? You know I'm not trying to get pregnant right now Jay, your ass is on papers and I'm not about to bring a baby in this world until you get your shit together." Diamond yelled. She was pissed off because he came inside of her.

"Bae we been together for five years, and you know I want kids by you so stop tripping! Damn I'm almost off papers and I'm finna retire from the game in a minute so you and our child will be straight. "Just chill." Jay said as he was making his way to the bathroom to shower so he could go to bed.

"What the hell ever Jay, you think I don't know you got to do some time, but I know. How long you got to do

Diary of a Triflin' Bitch

Jay? Be honest with me for once." Diamond was on the verge of tears. She hated the thought of being without Jay for one day and he felt the same about her, that's why he hadn't told her that he had to go do a year and a day. He had to go to court in two, and he was out grinding hard every night to get up enough money so Diamond wouldn't have to work while he was gone.

Jay hit play on the CD player in the bathroom to listen to some music before he got in the shower; this always relaxed him. Jay was a street dude but he loved R&B music. His mixed CD started to play Gerald Levert's "Definition of a Man." Jay lived by this song. He made sure Diamond didn't want for or have to ask for shit. Gerald Levert was one of his favorite artists; he called out to Diamond for her to come join him in the shower. "Diamond baby come on the water is just right for you, come here, let me rub you down." He knew it was going to be round two in the shower that's why he lit some candles and turned off the lights.

"Jay I know you heard me talking to you, how long are they offering you?" She said while she was getting in

Diary of a Triflin' Bitch

the tub with her man. No sooner then she got in the tub Jay's hands were all over her body. He had soaped up the sponge and was now bathing her in all the right places. He knew how to make her be quiet, so he rubbed the sponge between her legs as he placed one of her erect nipples in his mouth. Diamond released a moan of pleasure. That shit was feeling good to her. Jay knew he had her and that the conversation would be put on hold for another day. Jay rinsed her body off because he had to taste her again. Eating his woman's pussy turned him on. He was a man that believed in pleasing his woman at all cost. Jay raised her leg up on the tub as he made his way down south. Diamond had to find something to hold on to because she knew what time it was. Jay inserted two fingers inside of Diamond's nectar as he circled his tongue around her clit. He dug deep into her walls trying to find her g spot. Jay continued to suck on her clit until he couldn't take her screaming no more. He picks Diamond up with her back up against the wall and tongue fucked her until she came three times. After Diamond stopped convulsing and her legs stopped shaking Jay allowed her body to slide down the wall straight on his rock hard dick. His dick went right in because Diamond was so wet. Jay had Diamond's legs

Diary of a Triflin' Bitch

wrapped around his arms as he fucked her nice and slow. Jay kept plunging into Diamond's wet, hot box. Diamond couldn't take it anymore she was all sexed out. Jay felt her body tense up so he allowed her feet to hit the ground. Jay's dick was still rock hard, but Diamond knew what she had to do. Diamond got down on her knees and swallowed all nine inches of Jay's dick. She knew he loved this so she took her time in pleasing him. As she sucked Jay's dick she also played with his balls. Diamond had no gag reflex so it was easy for her to deep throat all of Jay's nine inches. Diamond clamped her throat down around Jay's dick and sucked him until Jay came. Diamond swallowed every drop of his babies; she loved the taste of her man's seed. She was very satisfied with her handy work. She got up and gave Jay a kiss. They bathed each other quick because Diamond forgot she had to go to work just that fast. Jay hated her working he wanted her to quit that damn job, but Diamond was very stubborn when it came to working. She always wanted her own money.

Diamond got out of the shower and entered their bedroom to get dress for work. As Jay was coming out of the bathroom Diamond was putting on her shoes. "Damnit

Diary of a Triflin' Bitch

bae you got to work again tonight?" Jay said mad as hell, he wanted to cuddle up with her until he went to sleep.

"Jay don't start that tonight, I only work three days a week so give it a rest please." She loved her man with every breath in her body.

"Why can't you just quit that damn job, I make enough money for us both you don't have to work bae, that's all I'm saying." Jay continued to get dress for bed.

"I keep telling you all money isn't good money, and your money is not promised to us if you got to keep doing time behind it." Diamond was done with this conversation she had to go. "Love you bae see you in the morning" Diamond turned and walked out the room.

She stopped by the guest room to check on Brandy before she left. She wanted to make sure her ass was asleep before she left the house, for some reason she just didn't trust her triflin' ass. "Brandy you sleep?" Diamond asked as she opened the door. Brandy didn't reply as she laid there mad as hell about the sex Diamond and Jay just had.

Diary of a Triflin' Bitch

She wished it was her in there getting dicked down. Diamond assumed Brandy was asleep so she just closed the door and went on about her business.

Diary of a Triflin' Bitch

Chapter 6

Brandy

Brandy waited until she heard Diamond's car pull out of the drive way before she got up out the bed and peeped out the curtains. She was thrilled to have Jay all to herself. She knew he didn't know she was there so her plan was to keep quiet until he went to sleep. She searched her purse for her pills to take one to calm her nerves. She had been prescribed an anti-psychotic for her Bipolar disorder that she had been diagnosed with since she was fifteen years old. She was taking Symbyax, it was an anti-depressant and an anti-psychotic combined. When she wasn't on her medicine her little friends would get her in a world of trouble. She swallowed her pill dry mouthed because she didn't have any water in the room. After she took her pill she laid down and dozed off. That's the only thing she hated about her medicine, they made her sleepy.

Meanwhile in the living room, Jay was having himself another drink as he was sitting on the couch

Diary of a Triflin' Bitch

flipping through the channels on the TV. He was bored as hell but he knew he would be asleep soon, because he was white boy wasted. He had been drinking and smoking all day, his home boys was trying to get him right before he had to go do his time. Jay stopped the TV on Bad Boys 2; this was one of his favorite movies to watch, it never got old to him. He really wanted to watch some of his 24 series, but he had made a promise to only watch it with Diamond. Jay and Diamond love Jake Bowers and would watch it almost every day together. He laughed and drank until he had passed out.

Brandy woke up from her sleep and heard the TV playing in the living room. She looked at the clock on the night stand and it read 3:34 a.m. She eased the door open to the bedroom and slipped down the hallway towards the living room. When she peeped around the corner she saw Jay's head back on the couch. She just stood there dazed for a minute or two before she finally realized he was asleep. Brandy's plan had come together. She could have her way with Jay and he wouldn't be able to do anything to stop her until it was too late. She took off all of her clothes in the hallway, she was ready to claim what her mind was telling

Diary of a Triflin' Bitch

her was hers. She knew she didn't have much time to get this job done because Diamond was due to get off at 6 a.m. Brandy eased further into the front room until she was standing in front of Jay butter ball naked. Her pussy was dripping wet from the thought of him being inside of her for the first time. Brandy got down on her knees and was thankful that Jay only had on some pajama pants; she eased his dick out of his pants and got the shock of her life. She was amazed at the size of him. Her mouth began to water as she slipped him into it. She sucked and sucked until he was hard as a rock. As she was sucking she reached down and started playing with her clit. She was ready to test the waters. She was very grateful it was dark in the room, so she eased his dick into her canal from the back. First she had to get use to the girth and length of him. She slide down on Jay's meat nice and slow, she had to get it wet with her juices. She had got about eight inches inside of her before she realized he was stretching her walls to the max. She moved slowly up and down on his dick until pain turned into pleasure and she started riding him harder. Jay didn't realize how drunk he was until he woke up to what felt like a wet dream. He was dreaming that he and Diamond were on a beach and she was putting it on him.

Diary of a Triflin' Bitch

Jay's mind said it was a dream, but his body was saying something different. He was awakened by a hard body riding his dick from the back. Jay tried to open his eyes but had a bad headache so he just enjoyed the ride. Shit was feeling good to him; he grabbed on to Brandy's body and held on firmly to her hips. Brandy's nipples instantly got hard from his touch, she put a smile on her face cause she knew he was too gone to know the difference between her and Diamond at that moment. Jay woke up and started knocking her back out, but Brandy had to find a way to control the situation cause the pain was back, he was not showing her any mercy. Brandy flipped around so she could ride him nice and slow from the front. As soon as she did that Jay's hand went straight up to her breast. He inserted one of her nipples in his mouth and Brandy let a moan slip out of her mouth. She thought for sure Jay would open his eyes, but at that moment he was so into getting another nut he was in a zone. Brandy wrapped her arms around his neck and started riding him harder. Jay took one of his hands and grabbed her ass to bring her down on his dick so he could go deeper. This was feeling so good to Brandy until she forgot who and where she was. Jay was now on the verge of busting and he started talk to her, "Bae

Diary of a Triflin' Bitch

I'm about to cum, shit this feels so damn good. Whose pussy is this? Huh? Oh shit bae I'm almost there! Can I please cum in you?" He yelled. Brandy screamed out in ecstasy "Yes boo do you! I'm finna cum too, cum with me!" Before her voice could register in his head he had busted a nut all up in her. When Jay opened his eyes it was too late to pull out of her.

"What the fuck are you doing?" Jay jump up knocking her on the floor as he was pulling up his pants.

"What's wrong with you, you wasn't saying that when you was just beating my back in!" Brandy yelled out from embarrassment. She was mad because in her little crazy mind she thought he was enjoying her.

"Bitch I thought you was Diamond. I would never have fucked you. Have you lost your damn mind? And how the fuck your funky ass got in here anyways?" He fumed.

"Oh, so I'm a bitch now, it's cool but now that we have did the deed you gonna pay me to keep my mouth shut or I'm telling Diamond you came on to me first. And

Diary of a Triflin' Bitch

she is gonna believe me after I show her the proof of what we just did nigga." Brandy had tears in her eyes as she yelled.

"Man get the fuck out of here with that bullshit, my girl ain't gonna believe nothing your stank ass has to say!" He was so mad he could have killed that hoe right then and there.

"You want to test me and find out pussy nigga? Ok let's do this, as soon as Diamond gets home I'm going tell her what just went down. She gonna be on my side because we have been friend since....."

Pop! Pop! Jay had leapt across the room to where she was and hit her in the mouth. That was one thing he didn't play was a mother fucker calling themselves threatening him. Before he knew it, he had his hands wrapped around her neck, and her feet were at least two inches off the ground. He had blacked out and he didn't release her until her eyes were rolling in the back of her head. He dropped her on the floor and stepped over her, so he was face to face with her. "Don't you ever threaten me

Diary of a Triflin' Bitch

hoe, now get the fuck up and get the fuck out of my house. If you so much as utter one word to Diamond about this, they will find your body floating in the Manatee River!" With that he ran up the stairs to go shower before Diamond got home.

It took Brandy ten minutes to get up and catch her breath. She was shocked at what had just happened. She had never been in a situation like this before but she had a plan up her sleeve. She gathered all of her clothes and went back in to the guest bedroom to retrieve the rest of her things. As Brandy was getting dress she realized that they had just had sex with no rubber on. Yes! She thought as she rushed to bathroom. She had to go check something out before she left the house. She sat on the toilet and inserted her fingers into her vagina and there it was, shit she was so caught up she forgot to take her nuvo-ring out. Her plan had failed this time but next time she would succeed. Brandy left Diamond's house and went and got a room at Days Inn. She needed a bath and some sleep to get her head together. When Brandy got to the hotel she realized she had left her diary at Diamond's house, "Shit! I have to go back and get that. If anybody finds it all hell is going to break

Diary of a Triflin' Bitch

loose. Man how the fuck am I supposed to get it now? Jay's ass don't want me back over there and he would kill me if I showed my face. I got to find a way to get my shit because if one of them hoes finds it they will kill me too once they read it. Brandy thought to herself.

Jay was just stepping out of his pajama pants when he looked down and saw Brandy's pussy juices all around his dick. "FUCK!" he yelled out in anger. He knew he had just fucked up big time. He knew then he had busted a nut up in her now he had to pray that the hoe didn't get pregnant. He had to keep tabs on her to see what was what. Jay entered the bathroom and didn't even turn on the CD player. He wasn't in the mood for music; he had murder on his mind. At that moment, he grew mad and sad all at the same time. Mad cause he knew he had to keep fucking with Brandy to see if she was pregnant and sad because if Diamond ever found out that would be the end of them.

Chapter 7

Jay

Jay was out picking up is money from all the trap houses he owned. Jay was riding around in his Dodge Challenger all black on black. He loved his car. Jay was now big time, so he felt he had to ride big time. Jay pulled his car in the driveway of his trap house on MLK. This house was a 3 bedroom 2 bath house that he owned. As he was getting out the car, he spotted a black beat up minivan easing up the street. In one split second he heard gunshots and hit the ground. POW, POW, POW Jay was frozen in place. He couldn't believe someone was shooting at him. The gunshots stopped and Jay tried to get up but couldn't move. He had been hit; his leg was burning bad but he knew he had to get up and move. Jay finally made it inside the trap house where his workers were. He had to see where the blood was coming from.

"Fuck! Who the hell was that? Y'all niggas got something to tell me?" Jay was in so much pain. All his

Diary of a Triflin' Bitch

workers were standing around just looking. One of his workers was already on the phone with the doctor. Nobody else said anything; they knew it was going to be hell to pay. What Jay didn't know was he had a trader in his camp that had set the whole shooting up. He wanted Jay's spot. Jay continued to yell out in pain. Jay's right hand man busted through the front door with his gun in hand ready to shot.

"What the hell happened, Jay are you alright?" Dayshawn asked while looking around the room. He wanted answers and he wanted them now!

"Yeah nigga I'm good, but I think I'm hit man. Nobody seen anything? What the hell I pay y'all for, not to be standing around. Y'all nigga better find out something before somebody loses their life." Jay vented, he was very pissed. He knew he had no enemies, either they called it a truce or they were dead simple as that. Jay never went to bed with an enemy lurking around. Dayshawn was looking around the room and noticed one of the workers was looking strange.

Diary of a Triflin' Bitch

"Aye Tee Tee, what's up man? Why you over there looking around like you crazy? You know who that was that shot up the spot?" Dayshawn wasn't one to play with he stood 6'3" and 240 pounds of all muscle. Tee Tee was scared shitless; he didn't want to tell what he knew because the person who set the shooting up was his cousin.

"Nawl Dayshawn, I don't know anything. I just never saw that much blood before." Tee Tee knew if Dayshawn or Jay found out that his cousin Ant set the shooting up it was gonna be either his life or Ant's life on the line. What Tee Tee didn't know was somebody was gonna die tonight so he better make a decision fast.

It took the doctor all of ten minutes to get to the spot to see what was going on. "Damn Doc you must have been right around the corner. What's good wit cha?" Dayshawn greeted the doctor.

"Yeah man I was eating dinner with my chick and you niggas fucked that up. Jay what's good wit cha?" Doc's real name was Leon but everyone calls him Doc.

Diary of a Triflin' Bitch

"Shit man this shit hurts, I think I'm hit." Jay yelled he was pissed off that someone would have the balls to shoot at him. He was calling a meeting because he had to get to the bottom of this shit.

"Let me see, looks like the bullet went through and through. You good I just have to stitch you up." Doc said he started to remove all of his equipment out of his bag.

"Aye Dayshawn call a meeting NOW! I need to get to the bottom of this." Yelled Jay. The room grew silent, everyone knew that Jay was going to kill somebody.

"I'm on it boss." Dayshawn stepped outside to call all five of their top lieutenants for the meeting. He looked at his watch it was now 2:43 p.m., so he set the meeting for 5 p.m. at the warehouse. All the niggas in their camp knew that when a meeting is called out the blue somebody fucked up and was gonna die.

Meanwhile back in the house, Tee Tee went out back and called Ant on the phone, "Aye nigga what the fuck was you thinking, the plan was to rob his chick not

Diary of a Triflin' Bitch

him. If this nigga finds out it was you, man we both dead!" He yelled as low as he could. He knew he couldn't be heard. He didn't even wait to listen to what Ant had to say, he closed his phone and went back inside the house.

Jay had notice Tee Tee had got missing but was too busy getting stitched up. He would put a bug in Dayshawn's ear as soon as he came back in the house.

"Alright man that does it for you. Take these for pain in a couple of day you will be straight. Your stitches are dissolvable so you don't have to get them removed. Try not to need my services any time soon, me and my lady friend is going on a lil vacation for the weekend." Doc laughed.

"Well my nigga we won't need you this weekend, but somebody gonna need a body bag!" Jay yelled. With that Doc left cause he didn't want any parts of the crime that was about to take place.

Jay was mad because he wasn't paying attention to his surroundings. His mind still was on the shit that

Diary of a Triflin' Bitch

happened with him and Brandy. He wanted to take care of her before he went to jail but now that shit had to wait until he got out. What he didn't know was that decision could be deadly to him.

Chapter 8

Tracy

"Tracy Everest." yelled the nurse. She had been waiting to be seen by the doctor for over an hour. Her appointment was at 3 p.m. and it was now 4:43 p.m. Tracy followed the nurse into the exam room.

"Hi." Tracy said to the nurse.

"Ms. Everest my name is Eva I will be your nurse today, we gonna need a urine specimen from you and the doctor will be in with your results. The bathroom is around the corner. I will be right back." Eva said and walked out the room. Tracy went into the bathroom to collect the urine specimen; she hated to go to the bathroom at this minute because she was burning down there and had a smell that would turn your stomach. She held her breath and collected the urine specimen. After she was done she washed her hand and then sprayed the bathroom with air freshener. She would hate for somebody to come in the bathroom after her

Diary of a Triflin' Bitch

and smell that. She had already shaved all the hair on her pussy off because she thought she had another outbreak of crabs.

Tracy walked back to her exam room to wait on the doctor, ten minutes later the doctor walked in.

"Hi Ms. Everest, my name is Dr. Sincere how's it going today?" He asked

"It's okay how are you?" Tracy answered back.

"It's been kind of busy today, any other concerns today that we need to address before I get to your results?"

"Yes, I have a smell coming from my lower area that makes me gag, and I think I may have crabs again." She stated while lowering her head. She was so a shamed to use the word again.

"Well Ms. Everest, we have checked you for all STD's are you ready for the results?" He asked while opening her file.

Diary of a Triflin' Bitch

"Ready as can be expected Doc." Tracy had to take a deep breath. She had been waiting on these results now for about two weeks.

" Well Ms. Everest, Hepatitis A,B,C are all negative, chlamydia and trichomoniasis was positive, herpes negative, crabs positive, HPV negative, syphilis negative, and HIV positive. I know that was a lot to take in, but do you have any questions?" The doctor said with some concern in his voice. He really felt sorry for the nineteen year old girl. Her life had just begun, now it was about to end.

"Did you just say I was positive for HIV?" Tracy was so shocked that was the only thing she had heard. She had HIV and only had one sexual partner in her life.

"Yes ma'am you were positive for HIV, chlamydia, crabs, and trichomoniasis. If you want to talk to a counselor, I can arrange it for you." His heart was breaking for her; he had a daughter her age. "You know you can still live a full life with HIV, as long as you take your meds." He felt he had to give her that last piece of advice.

Diary of a Triflin' Bitch

As the doctor was walking out of the room to go get the counselor, he looked back over his shoulder and saw the tears trailing down the young girls face. Tracy was stuck sitting on the exam table; she really didn't know what she was going to do. Only thing she kept hearing in her head was HIV. How could Dayshawn do this to her? Now she knew he had to die, that dirty dick bastard had to go.

As soon as she finished her thought a light skin woman came in, "Hi my name is Lisa Adams, do you want to talk about your status?" Tracy just looked at the woman with so much pain on her face.

"Can I get your card? I will call you when I'm ready to talk. This is too much right now; I got to go!" Tracy gathered all her belongings to leave.

"Yes Tracy, here is my card. My home and cell numbers are on the back of the card; please call me day or night for anything." Lisa wanted to make sure she kept in contact with this young girl.

Diary of a Triflin' Bitch

"OK Ms. Lisa I will thanks for everything. I will be in contact." Tracy said before walking out the room. She had to get up out of there; she was starting to feel like she couldn't breathe. On Tracy's hour and a half drive home, she had a heart to heart with herself. She made up her mind she was gonna kill Dayshawn.

Diary of a Triflin' Bitch

Chapter 9

Warehouse

As Dayshawn pulled his truck up to the warehouse, he noticed that all of their workers were there. He and Jay met at the back of the truck to talk before they went in.

"Hey man your lil homie Tee Tee...we need to press him about this here. Earlier he got missing for a minute or two and something isn't right about your boy. I think he knows who tried to set me up. Just watch his body language." Jay said looking in Dayshawn's eyes. At that moment he didn't trust anybody.

"Yeah man I got cha man; he was looking kind of suspect earlier. That nigga better be on the up and up or it's gonna be lights out for his ass." Dayshawn responded. Both Jay and Dayshawn knew what that meant, with that being said they both walked in the warehouse. It looked more like a party than a meeting.

Diary of a Triflin' Bitch

"Aye yo, what the fuck y'all niggas got going on in here. It's not play time in this bitch, get y'all selves together." Dayshawn yelled he was pissed off at the scene. Everybody got quiet when they saw the look on Jay's face. Dayshawn pulled a chair in the middle of the floor.

Jay took roll call, "Red, Tee Tee, Bone, Ant, Dayshawn, Zy, Kev, Poop, Jack, Quez, Ron, Boo Boo, Bay, Mike, Monte, Twerk, Man Man, Lil Rom, Jr, and Ice." As Jay called roll call he had everybody there except for Ant, Bay, Mike, and Kev. He looked at his watch and saw it was only 4:47 p.m., "These niggas got thirteen minutes or it was gonna be their asses" Jay thought. Jay went in the back room to call Diamond. "Aye bae what are you doing?" Jay said trying to feel her out to see what mood she was in before he told her he had got shot.

"Oh bae I'm on my way home to cook dinner so we can spend some time together. What time are you coming home tonight?" Diamond asked him.

"Well bae we got some shit going on right now that I got to get to the bottom of, somebody tried to set me up

Diary of a Triflin' Bitch

today. I got shot in the arm, I'm ok before you even start crying. So it's gonna be late when I get in. Bae I got to go, I will fill you in when I get home, you know I can't say too much over the phone." With that he hung up on her, Jay checked his watch he had seven more minutes before the meeting was to start. He went to go use the bathroom.

When Jay returned in the meeting room he noticed that everyone had made it in except for Ant. "Aye where the hell is Ant?" He asked Dayshawn but before he could respond Bay and Mike both said at the same time, "He left the spot earlier!"

"And he hasn't come back yet, I tried to call him but he didn't answer." Bay said.

"Man Jay he been MIA like all week, he would come to the spot for an hour or so then leave and don't come back." Mike added he knew somebody was finna die, and he didn't want it to be him.

"So why the hell y'all niggas ain't been said something?" Jay was pissed off, he knew something wasn't

Diary of a Triflin' Bitch

right, but Ant had made it to the top of his hit list. If that nigga didn't have a good reason why he wasn't putting in work, he had to die. "Alright let's start this here meeting. I will get up with that nigga later. First of all y'all niggas got my money for today's take?" Jay looked around the room. The way the room was set up was by trap house. The top lieutenant of every house stood up with a bag in their hand. Dayshawn walked around collecting the bags of money. When all the bags were collected Jay continued. "Tee Tee front and center!" Jay pointed to the chair in front of the room. Tee Tee had a look of shock on his face as he made his way to the front of the room. As soon as his butt hit the chair Jay backhanded him in the mouth. "Give me your fucking phone!" Jay screamed. It took Tee Tee a minute to get his self together; he reached in his pocket to retrieve his phone. Jay looked in the call log to check to see who he had been talking to. Little did Jay know Tee Tee had erased the call to Ant and had replaced it with a call to his mother?

"Where did you disappear to earlier today when I was getting stitched up?" Jay looked Tee Tee in the eyes and waited for a response.

Diary of a Triflin' Bitch

Tee Tee was scared to respond, with a shaky voice he answered, "I called my momma man."

"Isn't that nigga Ant some kin to you?" Asked Dayshawn, he was ready to shoot first and ask questions later.

"Yeah man, but I haven't heard from that nigga in a couple of days." Tee Tee really just wanted to get out the hot seat. Bay shot Tee Tee in the knee. POW! Echoed in the warehouse, this scared everyone in the room. They didn't know who was gonna be next. Tee Tee screamed out in pain holding his right knee.

"What the fuck you do that for?" asked Jay ready to shoot Bay. What Jay didn't know was that Bay overheard Ant on the phone talking to Tee Tee earlier.

"Man Jay that nigga lying, I heard Ant screaming Tee Tee name on the phone earlier, he said something about is the nigga dead then he left the house." Bay still had his gun aimed at Tee Tee.

Diary of a Triflin' Bitch

"Jay man I...... was the only thing Tee Tee could get out his mouth before Bay emptied his clip into him.

Jay looked around the room at everyone else, he was pissed he had a rat in his camp. He was too busy getting ready to go do his bid that he had let a lot of things slide. "Anybody else done switched sides? Speak now or forever hold your piece." Jay continued to speak, "I got $20,000 for that lil nigga head tonight, and I want him brought to me alive. Some of y'all may be wondering what's going on so here it is, I got shot at today and by the looks of it Ant and that nigga Tee Tee was the people who did it. If that thought ever crosses your minds this is what will happen to you." Jay and Dayshawn just walked out of the warehouse; nothing else had to be said. Only thing he was worried about was putting a bullet in Ant's head before Monday. Jay had to get home to Diamond; this was their last weekend together.

Chapter 10

Ant

Ant's phone kept ringing, but he refused to answer it. He knows now he had fucked up and had to get out of town if he wanted to live. Jay had sent the goon squad after him and he had been trying to call Tee Tee back but couldn't get an answer. That wasn't like Tee Tee not to answer or not return any of his calls.

"Man hurry the fuck up!" Ant yelled into the phone at Brandy. He just couldn't leave town without her. He was in love with her so she thought.

"I'm coming damn." Brandy hung up her phone. She text Dayshawn back to let him know she was getting ready to leave with Ant. Dayshawn knew how to get to Ant and that was through her. He had promised her five stacks if she led him to Ant. Brandy ran and got in the car with Ant. They finally pulled off, what Ant didn't know was pussy, was about to get him killed.

Diary of a Triflin' Bitch

"We got to go get this money from the safe house then we're out of here." Ant said. He was scared shitless.

"Cool, because I need my money. Why you say we got to leave town anyways?" She asked Ant, he had called her earlier after the call from Tee Tee but he didn't say too much over the phone.

"Well instead of waiting for that nigga to go to jail to rob his bitch, I tried to get at him today. But those lil niggas missed. Now he is looking for me. I think he already got to Tee Tee." Ant said.

"Nigga why y'all do that? Y'all niggas said y'all wasn't gonna move on this nigga until he was locked up!" Brandy said kind of loud. She had called Dayshawn phone before she got in the car, she had to make sure Dayshawn heard every word they said.

"Yeah I know, Tee Tee didn't even know about it, I had to make a boss move, so I made it." Was all Ant could say. But Brandy wasn't done with this conversation she had to make sure Dayshawn didn't link her to the set up.

Diary of a Triflin' Bitch

"Damn Ant, why the fuck you do that? I mean shit Jay was good to you and Tee Tee. He paid y'all good money to work for him." Brandy said laying it on thick.

This pissed Ant off, "Man shut the fuck up; I want to be the boss, and so a boss move had to be made." With that being said the car grew silent. Ant cut the music up in the car to let Brandy know that the conversation was over. They pulled up to the safe house and got out. As soon as they entered the house Brandy rushed into the bathroom. She hit end on the cell phone, erased her call log, flushed the toilet, and washed her hands before heading to the safe room. When she entered the room, Ant threw her a duffel bag for her money.

"You have three minutes to get your shit or I'm out of here." Ant said as he turned his back to continue to load all of his money in his bag. He wasn't planning on returning, so he got all of his money. Brandy proceeded to her safe, to get some of her money out. She wasn't planning on being gone that long so she just got half of her money out the safe. She was gonna wait until they got

Diary of a Triflin' Bitch

settled where ever they were going; then she would let Dayshawn know.

"Man lets be out." Ant grabbed his bag and walked out of the safe room. Brandy closed her safe and locked it. What Ant didn't know was that Brandy knew all of their safe codes, so she was planning on emptying out Tee Tee's safe when she returned. Ant made his way to I-75 and opened up his Chrysler 300 to 90 miles per hour heading south. He was Miami bound.

Meanwhile, sitting in the car Dayshawn and Bay had heard every word between Brandy and Ant. "Man where this nigga at?" Bay said, his trigger finger was itching he was ready to kill somebody.

"Aye man Brandy is my plug, just chill home boy. When they land and get settled where ever the hell they going she will call me or text to let me know where they at." Dayshawn had to try to calm Bay down; he had seen that look on his face many times before. He was feeling some type of way about the loyalty this nigga had for Jay.

Diary of a Triflin' Bitch

"Man your bitch better hurry the fuck up and come through or I'm gone look for this nigga my damn self!" Bay said before he jumped out the car and walked away.

Diary of a Triflin' Bitch

Chapter 11

Tracy

It was three in the morning and Tracy had been up now for more than 24 hours drinking and snorting coke. She just couldn't accept the fact that she was dying of HIV. She was on a mission, and that mission was to kill Dayshawn. He had been calling her all day, but she refused to answer her phone. It was now time for her to put her plan in motion; she pulled out her cell phone to send Dayshawn a text message. Her message read, *Hey, I've been busy lately. Sorry I missed your calls. Can I see you tonight?* She pushed send and waited for his response. Tracy drove to the next gas station she saw open, she needed some gas and some snacks. She had already got her supplies earlier that day, her plan was to stay the night with Dayshawn, cook dinner for him, then kill his ass. What Dayshawn didn't know was she had overheard his and Brandy's conversation the other day. She knew Brandy and Dayshawn had been sleeping together, but she just didn't know for how long. Brandy was next on her hit list. Tracy

Diary of a Triflin' Bitch

pulled her Lexus up to the gas pump. As she was getting out of her car, the dude next to her tried to holla at her.

"Hey Red, let me holla at you for a minute." He said to her.

"Nawl boo I'm already taken." Tracy stumbled to walk, she was high as hell. That coke and drink already had her gone. She proceeded to walk in the store where she grabbed a peach Nehi soda and a bag of chips. As she was making her way to the cash register, she notice the tall handsome dark skinned brother who had just tried to holla at her.

"Aye ma you just gonna dis a brother like that." He knew who she was; he was a jack boy and was trying to get close to Dayshawn and Jay. His name was Bo Peep.

"Boo I told you I was taken, but you can give me your number, and I will call you when I become single tomorrow. I feel you are taking up too much of my time tonight; I'm on a mission." Tracy rolled her eyes at him, paid for her items and gas then left out of the store.

Diary of a Triflin' Bitch

Bo Peep didn't care he already knew where to find Dayshawn, and he had written down her tag number. He had a chick that worked at the DMV so he would just have her look up Tracy's address. Bo Peep had seen the look in Tracy's eyes and knew murder was on her mind. It had just registered in his head what she had said; she was going to be single tomorrow. It was just his luck he could kill two birds with one stone. Bo Peep ran to go catch up with Tracy; he had to get more info and quick.

"Aye ma let me put a bug in your ear right quick." He said as he grabbed her arm and pulled her near him. Tracy crossed her arms and looked him in the eyes. Bo Peep knew he only had a little bit of time by the way Tracy was looking at him. "Aye I see you have murder in your eyes so I want to offer you my help. And by the statement in the store you got to want to kill that nigga Dayshawn. Am I right? I can help you with that." Bo Peep got straight to the point.

Tracy's mind was now racing; she wanted to know how the hell this tall sexy dark skinned man knew who her man was. But the part of him saying he could help her was

Diary of a Triflin' Bitch

more important to her. "How could you be of any assistance to me on that tip?" Tracy asked smiling.

"Well now that I got your attention your man got something I want and need so if you are trying to off that nigga I can help you with that." Bo Peep said hoping she takes him up on the offer.

Tracy looked Bo Peep in the eyes she could tell he was serious about this. She also could tell he wasn't the police by the way he talked, dressed, and his swag. "If you are serious about this, give me a call tomorrow morning and we could work out the particulars." Tracy said. She gave him her number and walked away.

Tracy finished pumping her gas she got into the car and checked her phone. She had two missed calls from Dayshawn and one text message also. She opened her text messages the message from Dayshawn read, *"Damn bae I've been trying to reach you all day. I will be home in thirty minutes. Bring yo ass, I miss you. Love you see you soon."* Tracy smile at the thought of her plan coming together. She text him back, *"I'm on my way be there in*

Diary of a Triflin' Bitch

twenty minutes." With that she put her car in gear and headed to Dayshawn's house. If this Bo Peep fellow worked out she wouldn't have to work so hard at killing Dayshawn. She would just put it on him tomorrow then use him in her plan.

Twenty-two minutes later she pulled her car in Dayshawn's driveway; Dayshawn hadn't made it home yet. It was okay because she had a key so she let herself in and went up the stairs to run the bath water. This was how they always started their nights off together every time they spent the night together. She put in his favorite CD in the CD player, made sure the temperature was right, poured some bath oil in the water, and went to get his favorite negligee out the drawer. By the time Dayshawn walked in she was completely ready to put it on him. That was the first part of her plan. Fuck him good tonight, and then tomorrow he had to die.

"Hey bae, are you hungry?" Dayshawn asked he had brought home some food from the Waffle House.

Diary of a Triflin' Bitch

"Sure I will be right down hold on a minute." Tracy had to get herself together. She was high, something she'd never been. She knew Dayshawn would be able to tell if he looked at her. She closed the bathroom door. Tracy took the coke out of her purse; she snorted two more lines then placed the rest of the coke under the bathroom cabinet. She didn't want Dayshawn to come across it. Tracy knew she was gonna need the coke to deal with Dayshawn; if she was sober she would probably kill his ass tonight. But she had the great plan and the perfect murder up her sleeve so she knew she had to chill. She then washed her face good and applied more makeup and lip gloss to her lips. She checked herself in the mirror to make sure she was good. Tracy made her way down the stairs. Dayshawn had just finished warming up their food.

"Hey bae you okay?" Dayshawn asked when he saw her walk into the kitchen. He had been worried about her. He knew he had given Tracy chlamydia and trichomoniasis, and knew she was on the verge of leaving him. Dayshawn knew he had fucked up by fucking that dirty bitch Brandy raw, but he was gonna make it right. After she lead him to Ant he was gonna kill her ass too.

Diary of a Triflin' Bitch

"Yeah bae, I just haven't been feeling good lately, I going to make me a doctor's appointment on Monday." Tracy said, but little did he know she already knew and it was on. She warned him the last time when he gave her crabs that if he gave her anything else she was gonna kill him. He would soon find out she wasn't playing.

"Okay do you want some soup instead of this?" He asked placing her plate of food in front of her. He felt bad that he was cheating on her. Once he got rid of Brandy he was planning on proposing to her. He knew from the very first day he met her, that she was a good girl. He just had to learn how to keep his dick in his pants.

Tracy wasn't really hungry, the coke made her lose her appetite. "Nawl bae I will eat this, I haven't really had nothing to eat all day. Thanks for thinking of me." She said.

"I know you and your ass is always hungry." Dayshawn laughed at his own joke. He had never met a woman so slim and can eat like her.

Diary of a Triflin' Bitch

"Boy shut up, you know me well." Tracy laughed back. They continued to have small talk until they were finished eating. Tracy had to keep talking to herself in her head; she really wanted to cut his throat.

"You finished eating bae?" Dayshawn asked he was being extra friendly to her.

"Yea I'm finna go up-stairs and warm our bath water." Tracy got up from the table as Dayshawn was clearing the table. She had to go hit her coke before Dayshawn got up stairs. She ran up the stairs as fast as she could. Meanwhile Dayshawn washed all the dishes and finished cleaning up the kitchen. He also went through his call log and erased Brandy's number, even though he had her number under a different name. He even erased two naked pictures she had sent him. Dayshawn couldn't let Tracy see that, he knew she would snap. As he was making his way out the kitchen, he turned off all the lights and made his way up the stairs. When he entered to room there were candles lit and music playing. He knew Tracy had to be in the mood to sex him good. Now he had to figure out how he was gonna put on a condom without her knowing it.

Diary of a Triflin' Bitch

He was already being treated for chlamydia and trichomoniasis and didn't want to be reinfected. Dayshawn opened the condom and placed it on his side of the bed; he would apply it as soon as he got out the bath tub.

"Bae come on before the water gets cold again." Tracy yelled from the bathroom. She was ready to get this part of her plan over with.

"I see you ready for daddy tonight." Dayshawn said as he made his way to the Jacuzzi tub. Dayshawn and Tracy took turns bathing each other. They took turns fondling each other for their own personal reasons. Tracy wanted to hurry up and get it over with and Dayshawn just didn't want the condom to dry out.

Diary of a Triflin' Bitch

Chapter 12

Brandy

Ant and Brandy had made it to Miami in no time. They got a hotel room for the night and would be looking for a house tomorrow. Brandy got the room in her name because Ant didn't want anything in his. He was already going to talk to Brandy about putting the house in her name also. As they got settled in their room Ant brought it up, "Hey Brandy tomorrow when we go get this house do you mind putting it in your name?" He asked her.

Brandy had to hide her excitement, now this was working out better then she expected. She would have all of this niggas money and a house to go with it. "That's cool bae, if that's what you want me to do." She damn sure didn't have a problem with it. Brandy smiled inside. Shit this was like taking candy from a baby.

"Yeah bae for right now I just don't want my name on anything. You know that nigga Jay can have somebody

Diary of a Triflin' Bitch

run my name and get any info he wants. So I got to sale my car to a private owner and we gonna get two new ones." He figured if he sold it to a private owner it couldn't be traced back to him in Miami.

    Brandy had to give him a hug for that last statement he just said, because she was on the verge of screaming. This nigga was dumber then she had thought. Ant thought the hug was cause he felt like he was taking care of her, but little did he know Brandy had a plan for that ass. The two of them had small talk for about twenty more minutes then Ant fell asleep. Brandy used this as an opportunity to send Dayshawn a text to let him know they were in Miami, and she would send him an address as soon as they moved in the house. She didn't care that it was six in the morning. The text read, *"Hey this nigga got us deep in Miami, we at a hotel for now. I will hit you up as soon as we move into our house. Love you."* Brandy pushed send and then erased the text message. She hadn't been taking her meds lately so her mind was telling her that Dayshawn would soon be her man, if she set Ant up.

Diary of a Triflin' Bitch

The next morning when they got up, Ant and Brandy both showered, dressed, and went out to go get breakfast. He had gotten up before Brandy and did a search of the area. He found a home that he knew she really would like.

"So bae how would you like to live on the beach?" He asked her as soon as their food came. He had to feel her out to see where her head was. He loved the ground she walked on, and he wanted to do anything to make her happy.

"It sounds great! Don't tell me you already found a house." Brandy smiled, "You did, OMG I want to go see it now!" She was so excited at the thought of owning her own home; she was thinking that was a perfect idea. She would have her house on the beach and all of his money. Now it was time to play her role as wifey.

"Wellll!" He paused for a big effect. Smiling he told her, "I already spoke to the real estate agent we meet with her at 11a.m. So eat up it's already 9:47 and we still got a forty-five minute drive." It took Brandy no time to finish

Diary of a Triflin' Bitch

eating her food; they were done eating and back in the car by 10:15. When they arrived to the house at 4424 N Bay Rd., Brandy almost choked on her spit. The outside of the house was the most beautiful thing she had ever seen. She had to slow down her breathing; it felt like her heart was going to pound out of her chest.

"Ant this can't be the house you found for us!" She screamed. Brandy jumped out the car before Ant could stop. She ran up to the door, it was unlocked so she walked into the foyer. "Hello is anybody here?" She asked before walking in slowly.

"Oh yes I'm in the kitchen, just hang a left at the next opening." The real estate agent said cheerfully. "Hi, my name is Emily how is your day going?" She said extending her hand to shake Brandy's hand. By this time, Ant had made it in the house.

"Hi, I'm Brandy, and this is my fiancé' Anthony." Brandy shook her hand. She had to make it sound good to the white lady. She really wanted Ant to get this house for her. Little did she know Ant had already spoken to the real

Diary of a Triflin' Bitch

estate agent ahead of time, he had met with her 8:30 that morning and signed the lease in his name. He wasn't worried about Jay finding him; coming to Miami was all a part of his plan.

"Nice to meet you both." Emily shook both of their hands; she played her part like she was getting paid to do. Emily had known Ant since he was a little boy; she was married to his uncle. Emily was just as hood as Brandy; she was the madam of her husband's organization she just worked as a real estate agent to help clean their money. " Well let's get started, about the house it was re-constructed in 2008, the interior is a spectacular elegant modern and open plan with minimalistic modern style furnishings as you can see. It has a full span sliding glass, and French doors that open to the widest bay view in all of Miami Beach. There are four queen size bedrooms with private en suite bathrooms; full second floor Grand Master Suite and terrace with an indoor Jacuzzi tub, sitting room, office and a private bar area. You all have a grand total of five bedrooms, six baths, and 5,758 square feet. Would you like to see the upstairs first?" Emily asked she was getting vibes from Brandy that she really didn't like. She was ready to

Diary of a Triflin' Bitch

get this over with. Emily showed them the rest of the house, signed the fake papers, gave Brandy the keys and then left. What Brandy didn't know was she just signed her papers stating she belongs to Black and Mild Elite for the next two years. Brandy saw the address listed on the paperwork, so she felt it was all good.

Emily usually doped her girls up, and then made them sign the contract. However Brandy was so happy to get a house she didn't even read over the paper work. What Brandy didn't know was her so call new house was already purchased for their forth hoe house. She would find out though.

"Okay bae now that that's done on to the car lot for our cars," Ant said. He was only going to buy one car today, and promised to go back to get her car, but that day would never come. Brandy was on cloud nine from today's events, she couldn't wait until Dayshawn came to kill Ant so the house and the cars could be hers. On their way to the car dealership Ant had to put his second part of his plan in motion, "Aye bae give me your phone." He said calmly. Brandy didn't want him to get suspicious so she just handed it to him. Ant made a left turn at the next street and brought the car to a stop at the very next stop sign. Ant rolled the window down and threw Brandy's phone out the of the car.

"What the fuck you do that for?" Brandy screamed; she didn't have anyone's number memorized but her girls and now she didn't know how she was going to get in contact with Dayshawn for the job. "Shit!" She thought. She knew he was up to something.

"Here," he said to her as he shoved the old looking flip phone towards her. Brandy look at the phone as if it had a disease. What the hell was she going to do with that?

"Man go head with that bullshit, what am I supposed to do with this?" She asked out loud this time. Brandy looked through the phone and saw only one number logged in the contacts.

"Look I got one too; we just have to lie low for right now. You already know what I'm up against back home. We can't contact anyone from back home until I figure out

Diary of a Triflin' Bitch

a way to get at Jay and Dayshawn. "Understood!" Ant raised his voice a lil. He had to start putting his foot down if he thought his uncle was going to let him run the house.

Brandy was kind of shocked to hear Ant raise his voice at her, he never spoke to her in that manner before. So she opted not to say one word. Brandy gazed out the window trying to come up with a plan now that she didn't have her phone. Ant looked over at Brandy and knew she was feeling some kind of way, but he really didn't care how she felt at this moment. He was tired of being played for a fool, so he repeated his self, "IS THAT UNDERSTOOD!" He yelled and hit the brakes for a good effect. Brandy's body jerk forward; she had to put her hands out in front of her so her head wouldn't hit the dash board.

"Yeah, damn." She said nervously, her voice was shaky, and she was scared that Ant was going to hit her. This terrified her, her daddy was very abusive that is one of the reasons she left home. Ant liked the reaction he got when he raised his voice. For the remainder of their ride to the car lot no one said anything. Both had things running

Diary of a Triflin' Bitch

through their heads, Brandy wanted to have nothing else to do with Ant and he had cash on his mind.

As they pulled into the car lot Ant gave Brandy some instruction, "When we get in here you don't say one word unless I tell you to, do we got an understanding?" He said through gritted teeth. Brandy couldn't do nothing but shake her head up and down, all the while thinking, *"This nigga done lost his everlasting mind! I really got to get the hell away from him before he starts to hit me."* Ant smiled to himself as he got out of the car, he loved the control he now had over her. For the last three years he had to play the chump role for his uncle so he could get close to Jay. Now he was back in his home town and he could be his self, and it felt damn good.

When he reached the door of the car lot, Ant looked back to see where Brandy was at, she was still sitting in the car. "Aye yo bring your ass on in here!" He yelled at her, Brandy was out of the car in 2.5 seconds. Damn, was all he could say to his self. The bitch could move fast if she really want to.

Diary of a Triflin' Bitch

Ant finished picking out his car and signing the papers in about an hour flat. Now only thing he had left to do was take this dirty bitch shopping for her some work clothes. He had to make sure she was going to be a top seller in BNM Elite, so he could get the million his uncle promised him for her. Hell he didn't think she was worth a million but cash is what it is.

"I'm going to follow you back to the house to park one of these cars, and then we are going shopping on me." Ant said in a very calm voice. This made Brandy perk up with a smile. She loved spending someone else's money it made her pussy wet just thinking about it. It was already after four so he had to hurry up. He was still trying to make it to the KOD tonight, which was his first meet with his uncle so he couldn't be late. He gave her the directions on how to get back to the house. Ant got into his new 2014 Dodge Challenger cocaine white on white; he was feeling like he was a real boss.

They made it back to the house with no problem; Brandy was wondering how the hell Ant knew how to get around so good in Miami. She was sure to ask him as soon

Diary of a Triflin' Bitch

as she got back in the car with him. Brandy pulled the car in the garage as she was told. Ant waited until Brandy got in the car before he pulled off heading to Aventura Mall.

    Brandy got in the mall and went crazy; she had Ant from one end of the mall to the other. They went to Macy's, Bloomingdale's, Abercrombie and Fitch, Banana Republic, Rainbow, Body Central and of course Victoria Secrets. By the time they got finished shopping Ant was out of twelve stacks. He considers it an investment so he was cool with that amount. When Brandy got in the hoe house her first payment would be that $12,000. They grabbed something to eat from the mail and then headed back to the room where they got dressed and step out.

Chapter 13

The Hospital

Beep! Beep! Beep! That was the only sound heard in the room. The doctors and nurses had been working around the clock on this unknown man for the last sixteen hours. They had finally gotten him stable enough to where they felt he would live. The doctors had pulled six bullets out of him; they weren't for sure if he was going to make it or not. He had no ID on him when he was brought in, so he was listed as a John Doe. The only thing keeping this man alive was life support. The doctors didn't know what else to do for him. They had no family to contact for the patient. They had him in ICU so he could be watched around the clock. Doctors didn't know what happen to him, but what they didn't want was for whoever did this to him to come back and try to finish him off.

"Hey Nurse Adam, how is our patient doing?" The charge nurse asked the other nurse on duty to get an update on him. She knew it wasn't any change but she still had to

Diary of a Triflin' Bitch

ask. It was proper protocol at the hospital to give a report every hour on the hour for patients in ICU.

"Hey Miss Lady, how are you doing tonight?" Adam asked. He had a crush on his charge nurse but didn't know how to tell her. So he tried to do his best work when he knew he was going to be working with her. "There really isn't much change, his vitals are still stable. BP 130/82, pulse 83, and temperature is 98.9. How are we doing on finding his next of kin?" Adam wanted to know how far they were on getting that info because he felt so sorry for the young man, and he wanted to gain cool points for showing some concern. He used to be in the dope game but turned his life around after a near death experience.

"Well Adam, the hospital is keeping this one quiet; we don't know who is after this young man so we are not releasing any information on him. The press doesn't even know about him being here, and we would like to keep it that way." The charge nurse said to him while looking him straight in the eyes. Adam understood every word she had said. "Well, I'm going to go in and check him over before I

Diary of a Triflin' Bitch

go home for the morning, if you would like to go take a break you can. I will watch him for you." She said to him.

"Hey thanks, I do need some coffee and a smoke break if you know what I mean. Give me about ten minutes, I will be right back." Adam gathered his stuff and then left. Only the employees he was cool with knew about his weed habit.

The nurse went on in the room and did her thing; it took her all of twenty-five minutes to check and recheck him again. The nurse emptied out his catheter, brushed his teeth, lotion his skin, and prayed over him. As she made her way out of the room to the door of his room she said in a whisper, "Tee Tee please pull through this bae. Our unborn child is depending on you. I can't do this by myself. You told me that if I left Jay we could be together. Boo who did this to you? Wake up and tell me who put you in here. I love you." Diamond said before she walked out of the room.

Diamond and Tee Tee were high school sweethearts, but she left him when she met Jay. She

Diary of a Triflin' Bitch

thought because he was older than her he was going to treat her right. Not! She soon found that not to be true, she knew about the other woman he was sleeping with and making house with. But Tee Tee always was going to have a piece of her heart. She and Tee Tee ran into each other one night she went to the trap house to go pick up Jay. That's how she found out he was working for Jay and the rest is history. Now she was pregnant and her baby daddy might die.

As Diamond made her way back to the nurse station so she could do her report, Adam was walking up the hall, "So Miss Diamond when are we working together again?" He tried to make small talk but Diamond wasn't up for it.

"Goodnight Adam I got to go. Take care." With that being said she walked away and left the hospital.

Diary of a Triflin' Bitch

Chapter 14

Tip

Tip was sitting in her den trying to get in contact with her sister, she hadn't heard from her in three days. Every time she called her cell it went straight to voicemail. She was trying to see what the hell was going on with their money, the set up and if Jay was dead. Tip hadn't spoken to Terry; he really hadn't been home for the last three days so she knew something was going on. Terry was Jay's connect so when Terry's money wasn't right he didn't come home.

"Aye bitch this my fourth time calling you, answer your damn phone!" Tip screamed into the phone. Five minutes after Tip sat the phone down it rung; she snatched it up and answered it without looking at the caller ID.

"Aye, how are you doing today Miss Lady?" The voice on the other end of the phone said. Tip instantly got chills as she looked at her phone. The call said unknown caller. Tip placed the phone back to her ear as she now knew who was on the other end.

Diary of a Triflin' Bitch

"You not talking to me?" Akeem said into the phone; he was smiling at the thought of the fear he had over her. Their agreement was that either she would set up Terry to be robbed, or she would become one of his slaves. He had already planted his seed in her so it was going to be a piece of cake.

"Akeem how are you doing hun?" Tip tried to sound as if she was happy to hear from him. That couldn't be any further from the truth though; she was scared to death to be in the same room with this man.

"It's that time! I need my money. When can I come get my money or my woman? It's time to collect." Akeem said into the phone. He was done playing with Terry he needed his money. Or Tip was going to have to work it off.

"You got to give me more time; I'm trying to get in contact with my sister now. We are working on it together, when she calls me I will call you I promise." Tip said with desperation in her voice. She needed more time because she really didn't want to become his slave again.

Diary of a Triflin' Bitch

"Don't worry about your sister! She is now my ransom until I get what I want! She now works for me." Akeem started to laugh an uncontrollable laugh.

"NOOOOOOOOOOOO! Fuck" Tip screamed as she threw her phone across the room. She knew at that moment shit had gotten real. Now she didn't have anybody; see she was always out for self-getting over on people. So now that her sister was gone she had to figure out how to get her back. Tip knew it was going to be a hard task but she had to come up with something.

See Tip had met Akeem one night when her and Brandy was out at the club. He looked like money, smelled like money and fucked her like money. First he would ask her to do little things like, a threesome, sex parties, his home boys, you name it he made her do. It wasn't until after he had her caught up in his little web that it was too late to leave him alone. Before she knew it, he had her stripping, turning tricks, on meth and his sex slave.

"Terry where the hell are you? Get your ass home now!" Tip yelled at his answering service. Terry hadn't

Diary of a Triflin' Bitch

been answering his phone either. Tip wasn't going to just sit around the house and wait for Brandy to get killed behind her, so she grabbed her purse and keys to go find Terry. Her plan was to get Terry on her team to help find Brandy and set him up all at the same time.

Chapter 15

Tracy

Tracy was out and about doing some running around for her plans for tonight. Dayshawn had some meetings today, so that gave her time to set everything up. First stop was to the dopeman's house; she needed some coke for herself and some LSD to spike Dayshawn dinner. She also was going to mix it with a lil rat poison to make sure the job got done. She had to drive to a different city to get her dope because all the trap houses in Jacksonville were owned by Jay and Dayshawn. She had learned about this certain trap house through Brandy; she used to date one of the dudes that used to trap out of the house. However he met his untimely death at the hands of Brandy, Tee Tee and Ant. Tracy walked to the door of the trap house and knocked.

"Who the hell is it this early in the morning? These damn fiends are up early as hell." Yelled Max to his home boy from the other side of the door. It was only 8:30 in the morning. Their shift was almost over, and he was tired.

Diary of a Triflin' Bitch

"Tracy." She yelled trying not to sound so nervous. This dude had a very deep voice and it scared her. Tracy heard music playing through the door. She was about to walk away when the front door swung open.

"What! Oh Shit! Excuse me Miss Lady what can I do for you this fine morning?" Max said trying to flirt with this beautiful lady standing in front of him. The site of Tracy made his dick hard.

"Umm my home girl told me this was where I could come to get some good blow." Tracy said with shakiness in her voice. This dude was standing about 6'7'' and weighed 250 easy. Tracy almost pissed on herself.

"Aye who is your friend? And what are you looking for and how much?" Max said looking behind Tracy making sure everything was ok. They had been robbed three times before and weren't trying to get robbed again.

"Her name is Brandy; I'm looking for some coke and liquid LSD or pills. I need an eight ball of coke and a

Diary of a Triflin' Bitch

half a liter of LSD or fifty pills." Tracy said pulling out her money.

Max looked at her suspiciously for a minute then out of nowhere he snatched her money out of her hand to count it. She had given him $450. "Your count is right, but you need an extra fifty bucks for such a short notice on the pills and we don't carry liquid. The eight ball will run you $200 and the pills are $250." Max said while still holding his hand out for his other fifty dollars.

"Cool." was all Tracy could say. She was willing to give him any amount he wanted. For one, she didn't know how much her dope was supposed to cost her and two she was ready to get the hell away from this big black ass giant. She passed him the other $50 dollars.

Max slammed the door in her face as he went in the house to get her drugs. Tracy didn't know what to think. She stood on the porch, waiting with a lot of thoughts running through her mind. Seven minutes later the little slit in the door came open and scared the piss out of Tracy. The

Diary of a Triflin' Bitch

drugs were dropped through the slit of the door and just as quick as it opened, it was closed.

Tracy picked her drugs up off the ground and ran back to her car. As she secured herself in her car; Tracy's heart tried to return back to normal as she was backing out of the driveway. Tracy drove down the road as far away from the house as she could get before she pulled over to put her drugs in the trick compartment under the arm rest. Tracy's heart still was pounding in her ear drums she was scared as hell of Max. Tracy hit her coke to try to calm down.

After Tracy got herself together she continued her ride back home; her phone rung she looked at the caller ID and didn't recognize the number so she didn't answer it. The only thing on her mind was killing Dayshawn. Tracy's phone rang again with the same number popping up and this annoyed the hell out of her. Whoever this was calling was very persistent about getting in contact with her, but she didn't care she was high as hell and didn't feel up to talking to anybody. Tracy turned her radio up to tune out the ringing phone. This helped Tracy calm down a little and

Diary of a Triflin' Bitch

made her ride home a lot smoother. As Tracy was pulling into Dayshawn's driveway, she noticed that she had seven missed calls. When she checked them she had five from a number she didn't know and two from Dayshawn. Tracy took a deep breath as she pushed send on her cell phone, "Hey baby how's it going out there for you today?" Tracy asked in her sweetest voice.

"It's going good bae, what are you up to today? Did you go to the doctor?" Dayshawn asked trying to see where her head was.

Tracy rolled her eyes in her head she knew what Dayshawn was doing and was so glad she had something nice planned for his ass. "Nawl bae my appointment is scheduled for next Tuesday at 2 p.m. But I've been out shopping getting everything ready for our special night together. What time are you coming home tonight so I can have your dinner ready and hot?" She asked

"Well I'm going to try to be there by 9 p.m. Shit has been crazy for the last few days. Jay has to go turn himself in tomorrow, so I have to step up my game if you know

Diary of a Triflin' Bitch

what I mean. I gotta go meet up with your girl later, but after that I will be done." Dayshawn explained without saying too much over the phone.

"Sounds good bae. I'm cooking your favorite tonight so make sure you have your ass home. I got a very special night planned for us it's to die for." Tracy smiled at her own joke.

"Daddy will be home as soon as I can, I can't wait to see what it is my baby has planned for daddy." Dayshawn's dick got hard at the thought of what Tracy was going to do to him. She could be a bit of a freak when she wanted to.

"Okay bae I'm getting another call but what kind of wine do you want to go with your dinner? Do you want white or red wine?" Tracy said trying to get Dayshawn off the phone he was making her sicker by the moment. She hated this man for ruining her life but pay back is a bitch!

"Bae it doesn't matter, you choose the wine. It's almost five o'clock so let me go finish my work so I can get home to you. I will see you around nine." Dayshawn said before he hung up the phone.

Tracy went in the house to get started on their dinner and once she had everything on she went in the bathroom to shower and shave. She wanted everything to be ready for her last night of passion with the man that she loved and hated. Tracy took her time in the shower so by the time she was finished it was already 6:30. Tracy finished cooking in her bath towel since there was no need to get dressed right now. Dinner was done by 7:15 so she had enough time to get the other part of her plan together. By 9:00 Tracy was done cooking, dressed in Dayshawn's favorite catch me/fuck me dress, and had soft music playing.

As Dayshawn entered the house he noticed the lights were off, but didn't question it because he saw the rose petals and candles leading him to the dining room. A smile came across his face when he saw Tracy walking out the kitchen with his plate of food and his glass of wine in her hand. "Damn bae you did all of this for me? What's the

Diary of a Triflin' Bitch

occasion?" Dayshawn took off his jacket so he could sit and enjoy his dinner.

"This is a just because dinner. Go ahead and wash up while I go get my food." Tracy said. As Dayshawn walked away Tracy went to work; she pulled the tissue from her bra. She had crushed ten of the pills she got earlier and she poured half in his wine and the other half in his food. Once everything was stirred up good she went ahead in the kitchen to get her food and the rest of the wine. Tracy was sitting and eating when Dayshawn returned. "Bae what took you so long?" Asked Tracy as Dayshawn walked back into the room.

"I had to make a couple of phone calls before I turned my phone off for the night. Now, I'm all yours. Damn bae this looks and smells good!" Dayshawn said as he dug into his food. Little did he know this was the last meal he would be eating before he went to take his long dirt nap.

"Are you sure you are done for tonight; I want you all to myself. You have been busy and so have I. I need

Diary of a Triflin' Bitch

your undivided attention." Tracy said trying to sound sweet.

"Okay bae the phone is off and I'm all yours from the rest of the night." Dayshawn said as he continued to eat. They talked about everything under the sun from them getting married to how they were going to put it on each other after dinner. Conversation was good between them until Dayshawn started to sweat and then passed out face first in his plate. Now it was time to put her plan in motion.

Diary of a Triflin' Bitch

Chapter 16

The Trade

"Make it rain trick, make it, make it rain trick." The latest Travis Porter song blasted. King of Diamonds was on fire and money and ballers were everywhere in the club. Ant and Brandy were early for his meeting with his uncle. They got a table and ordered drinks. Brandy was on her second drink when she got the urge to go to the bathroom.

"Hey Ant I'm going to the bathroom; you want me to stop by the bar to get you another drink?" Brandy asked as she stood up.

"Nawl but hurry your ass back here, don't get lost. I need you to be here for this meeting with my peoples." Ant said rolling his eyes at her while looking around the club for his uncle. He couldn't wait until he sold her ass off. Being around this bitch was becoming more of a battle for him. The one million he was supposed to get from his uncle was well worth him having to deal with her nasty ass.

Diary of a Triflin' Bitch

Brandy walked away never noticing the dark skinned man in the corner looking at her. She was so into getting away from Ant for a few moments that she really didn't care who was looking at her. She needed to meet her a quick lick to get her money up so she could get away from his now controlling ass. Now she was starting to regret leaving all her money in the safe back home. Brandy went and stood by the bathrooms to just survey the club; she noticed ballers, scrubs, and a lot of wanna-be's throughout the club. She made eye contact with a couple of dudes and was on her way to go talk to one when she was backed handed out of nowhere. "What the…" Brandy couldn't even get the words out before she was hit again this time with a closed fist. Now she was terrified. She looked up into the eyes of a man she didn't even know.

"You didn't go in the bathroom so what you doing over here? Get back to the table." The man said and then walked away. Brandy ran her ass back to the table where Ant was supposed to be sitting. She just stood there looking around trying to see where he went to. She knew she didn't want to be standing in that corner just in case the crazy man came back. Everybody in the club was in their own world

Diary of a Triflin' Bitch

and wasn't worried about the fight that just happened by the bathroom. And for the ones who did see it they just thought it was a pimp checking a hoe that got out of line.

Ant and his uncle were standing on the far side of the club watching Brandy as she looked for him. His uncle had put him on game about her movements, "Unc what you do that for?" Ant asked about the altercation that just happened.

"Keep your bitch in check." His uncle said and headed to the bar. Akeem was just trying to show his nephew how hoes could get out of line in public. Ant walked back over to the table where Brandy was standing.

"Where have you been? I've been looking for you all over this damn club! Some crazy ass man hit me for no reason, I'm ready to go. Now!" Brandy screamed in his face. This really pissed him off. Ant pulled back and hit Brandy with all his might. He knew his uncle or his uncle goons were watching him. Brandy was sick of people hitting on her but what could she do.

Diary of a Triflin' Bitch

"Who the hell are you talking to for one? You better watch your damn tone before you lose some of your pearly white teeth. And two your ass was supposed to go to the bathroom and bring your ass straight back! I told you I had a meeting and you needed to be at the table, but no you was all over there by the bathrooms scoping the place out. What you got up your sleeve?" Ant said in her face. He was just about tired of her mouth and was ready to have her ass on alligator alley somewhere. Brandy was speechless. She really didn't know what to do. *What the hell did I get myself into? This nigga done changed on me. He never used to act like this before,* Brandy thought to herself.

"I'm just saying can we please go home cause my head hurts. Some dude slapped the shit out of me and now you just hit me. Bae I'm sorry for talking to you like that it will never happen again." Brandy said trying to smooth things over with Ant. The way she figured if she played along with this game he was now playing it would be less pain on her.

"Man I'm not trying to hear all that sorry shit; sit your ass down and wait until I have my meeting. We are

Diary of a Triflin' Bitch

not leaving until then. Do I make myself clear?" Ant asked through clenched teeth. Brandy had never seen that look in his eyes; he looked evil. Brandy shook her head up and down while taking a seat in her chair. She just couldn't believe how the tables had turned on her. She was always in control of the situation so she thought. Brandy looked up and saw the same man who had slapped her over by the bathrooms walking their way. She tried to tell Ant again but was hushed up with a look that said if you say one word I will fuck you up.

"You ready to start this meeting?" Asked Akeem as he walked up to Ant and gave him some dap like they already knew each other.

"Yeah man I'd like for you to meet my chick Brandy. And Brandy this is Akeem." Ant said as he watched Brandy squirm in her chair.

"Very nice to meet you beautiful lady." Akeem said in his most charming voice. Brandy just looked at Ant for the okay to speak back. She didn't want to be hit again. Ant gave her a head nod signaling that it was okay.

Diary of a Triflin' Bitch

"Hi." Brandy said dryly. This man had her confused. She really wanted to know what was going on between Ant and this man and why the hell did he hit her. But also his swag was hypnotizing to her; the way he talked she knew he had money, and his eyes were empty. She knew he was nothing to be played with and she didn't want to be in the same room with this man.

"Now that we got that out the way," Akeem said with a smile on his face. He pull out the contract Brandy had signed earlier and placed it on the table, "As stated in this here contract you belong to me now." He said pointing at Brandy. "Work starts tonight. You looking good I know you can make me a couple of thousand tonight."

Brandy was speechless her mind was racing; she didn't remember signing no contract. And what did he mean by she belong to him. OMG! What the hell was going on here? Is that why he hit me? He thinks I'm one of his girls. "What contract…" was all she said. Ant gave her a look of death. She now knew her place.

Diary of a Triflin' Bitch

"Is the price still the same Unc?" asked Ant. He had slipped by calling Akeem Unc but he wanted to make sure he was going to get his money.

"Yeah son you can go on over there by the bar and Zeek will give you a briefcase. Let me get well acquainted with Ms. Brandy here and give her the rules. You know the do's and the don'ts." Akeem was enjoying the look of horror on her face. Zeek was Akeem son and right hand man; he had groomed him to be a killer at all cost. Ant shook hands with his uncle, gave Brandy a kiss on the cheek then whispered in her ear, "Thank for being the nice, nasty ass bitch you were, you wanted to be a hoe now I sold your ass like the hoe you are. See you later." With that being said he walked off to get paid.

Brandy was in tears she really didn't know what to do now. Did Ant sell her to this man? What did he mean by making a couple thousand tonight? Was she now this man's slave? Brandy was in total disbelief at the thought of being someone's sex slave.

Diary of a Triflin' Bitch

"Don't cry now Ms. Brandy; we got money to make. Here are the rules: you are to do what you are told at all times or you will be punished. Your contract says you belong to Black and Mild Elite entertainment for the next two years. Your new job is to be my hoe. You are not to bring home anything less than three thousand a night. If you do you will be punished. You have less than five minutes to go in the bathroom to get yourself together, take your panties off, and get ready for your new daddy to try his candy out. Are we clear? And don't try anything slick I already have eyes on you so do as you are told, and you won't get hurt anymore." Akeem snapped his fingers and one of his men grabbed her by the arm and led her to the bathroom.

Akeem went to go find Ant to have a couple more words with him about their deal, then on to the bathroom for some head and some ass. He had to make sure the product was right for his people.

"Aye nephew are you good?" he asked.

Diary of a Triflin' Bitch

"Yeah man everything looks good, but about the other thing we talked about, you know the job. I can't go back to where I just came from. Them niggas is looking for me so I need you to put me on. I would like to run the new house you and Emily have. What you think?" Ant said with desperation in his voice. He really needed that job.

"If you want it nephew you can have it. I mean I do have to talk it over with Emily tonight, but I'm pretty sure she will agree. Welcome home nephew I told you once you got back I would have a job for you. I got to run so I can get your girl in line but before I go let me ask you this. Will it be a problem for you working with Brandy or should I put her in a different house? I will not stand for either one of you messing up my money." Akeem asked seriously.

"Nawl Unc I'm good on that end, that hoe don't mean shit to me now. She tried to set me up the bitch is all yours. She better not get out of line or I'm going to bust her ass." Ant said louder than he tried to.

"Calm down nigga. Get with me tomorrow I got some things to go over with you about running the house

Diary of a Triflin' Bitch

and about those niggas you were running with. We don't need any problems. Say we meet bout 9 a.m. for breakfast at IHOP." Akeem said looking at his watch he had less than two minutes to get to the bathrooms. He was ready to get his dick sucked.

"Cool Unc I'm going to stay at the house tonight I don't want to go back to the hotel." Ant said.

"Nawl nigga nobody is staying at the house until we get it furnished. You go on back to your hotel and you can pick two girls to take with you on the house, for tonight only. After tonight no more fucking the girls you got that?" Akeem asked. That was one of his rules, no fucking the girls in the camp at all, but tonight was special for Ant so he had to let him get a taste test.

"Alright Unc I'm out." Ant said and walked away fast because he really needed some pussy. Ant picked two of the thickest girls he could find that were standing over by his uncle goons. One dark skinned and the other was mixed. Ant and the girls walked out of the club and headed to a different hotel. He had money to blow and refused to stay in that dump of a hotel him and Brandy were staying in.

Chapter 17

Jay

"Man fuck this shit I'm not going, them crackers gonna have to come get me. I got to find this nigga Ant. Hell we already got that nigga Tee Tee. I still need to find out who else was in on this set up." Jay said to Diamond. He had to report to the county jail today. But now he was trying to buck. That statement about them getting Tee Tee pissed Diamond off to the tenth power. She was glad Jay wasn't looking at her. Diamond really didn't have time for his bullshit today, she had less than two hours to get him there and get back to the hospital to Tee Tee. He was doing really well and the doctors were talking about taking him off the ventilators today.

"Look Jay, we already talked about this shit. If you don't turn yourself in today you can kiss me and your unborn child goodbye. I refuse to bring this baby in the world knowing you are on the run. Not going to happen. You can always get Ant later or what the hell do you have goons for if those niggas can't get him for you. Shit don't make no damn sense." Diamond said walking into the bathroom. She had been having morning sickness all morning, she didn't know if it was the baby or just knowing she was going to be rid of Jay for good.

Jay sat on the edge of the bed replaying Diamonds words in his head. He really didn't want to lose his family over some street beef with a young nigga. It was time for him to man up, he had to go lay down. If he ran he knew they were going to give him more time than a year and a day. "Okay bae I feel you on that. Promise me you're going to take care of yourself while I'm gone. Oh yeah you don't have to go do the pickups either somebody from my camp will either bring the money over here or to your job every day. Make sure you put it up somewhere but not in this house cause I would hate for somebody to run up in here and rob you." Jay said as Diamond was coming out of the bathroom. He had already paid the rent up for the year he was going to be gone. When he found out Diamond was pregnant, he changed his original plan quick. He didn't want her making pickups while she was carrying his child.

Diary of a Triflin' Bitch

"Aye why don't you get your girl Brandy to come stay with you while I'm gone so you won't be in this house by yourself?" Jay asked. He really didn't care for Brandy but he knew she was Diamond's friend and he didn't want to leave his pregnant girlfriend in the house all by herself.

"Maybe I will but I think I will be fine by myself in this house Jay." Diamond said trying to make him feel like he was running shit but in fact she wasn't going to stay there either. Once Jay turned himself in she was moving out into a new apartment she had rented.

"Okay, bae lets go before I change my mind again. I hate this shit man. Fuck!" Jay screamed as he walked out the bedroom heading downstairs. The more he talked about it he was having second thoughts about going to jail. Diamond noticed it too, so she wasn't going to say nothing else about it. She was just ready to drop his cry baby ass off. She had never seen a nigga whine about going to do some time.

"I'm ready when you are bae. I will meet you in the car." Diamond made sure everything was cut off in the

Diary of a Triflin' Bitch

house before she walked outside to the car. Jay's whining was really making her sick she had to hurry up and get away from him. Diamond was sitting in the car listening to her music for what seemed like forever, but it was only about ten minutes. Diamond blew the horn signaling that she was ready to go. Jay came outside with a cup in his hand. He had to get his last drink in and also call Dayshawn, that nigga hadn't been answering his phone. "Did you make sure the door was locked?" Diamond yelled out of her window.

Jay turned around to double check the door before he got in the car. "The door is locked bae. Have you heard anything from your girl Tracy today?" He asked her.

"Nawl why, what's up?" Diamond asked as she put the car in gear and pulled out of the driveway. "I haven't talked to her in a couple of days." Diamond was now thinking how she could let so many days go by without talking to her friend.

"Well, Dayshawn said he had to go home early because Tracy was cooking him dinner, and they were

Diary of a Triflin' Bitch

going to spend some time together. Now the nigga ain't answering his phone. Your girl must have put it on that nigga last night." Jay said as he tried Dayshawn's phone again but got the voicemail. "Fuck it. When that nigga gets in contact with you let that nigga know that I said he needs to come see me ASAP." Jay said as he turned the music up in the car. He felt like something was wrong with his boy but he didn't have time to go check on him.

"After I drop you off I will go by there and holla at him for you." Diamond said trying to make him feel at ease. Jay put in his favorite CD, closed his eyes and grabbed Diamond's hand and just relaxed in his seat. He had so much shit rolling around in his head he didn't know what to say to Diamond. "That's why you my baby you always got my back. I love you Diamond I hope this time apart pulls us closer. When I jump, we're getting married." Jay said before he closed his eyes again.

Diamond didn't say anything she just listened to him talk. She loved Jay, but she was in love with Tee Tee. She knew once Jay found out about her and Tee Tee he was going to put a hit out on her and him. As far as she knew

Diary of a Triflin' Bitch

nobody knew Tee Tee was still alive and she planned on keeping it that way. Thirty minutes later they were pulling in the county jail parking lot. Diamond turned the radio down, "Well bae this is it." Diamond said with tears in her eyes she already knew this was the end of them.

"Bae don't cry I will only be gone for a minute. We can do this man. Clean your face and give your man a hug. You don't need to be stressed out about me I will be alright. Promise me you are going to take care of yourself." Jay said as he wiped his eyes too he hated to see Diamond cry. They had been through a lot together this was just a little bump in the road that they had to cross.

"I promise bae please take care of yourself in there." Diamond's face was now soak and wet from her tears. She was in so much pain partly from the thought of being free from Jay's hold, but the other part of her was in pain from the thought of her having to be on the run from Jay for the rest of her life.

"I love the both of you." Jay said as he leaned back so he could rub on her stomach. He had to do the right

Diary of a Triflin' Bitch

thing if he wanted to be there for his child. He was really thinking about leaving the game for Diamond and his unborn child. Jay looked at his phone and noticed he only had about ten more minutes to be inside before they issued a bench warrant for him. He couldn't have that because that would be another charge.

"When are visiting days and hours?" Diamond asked trying to act like she really cared. She was only going to visit him until Tee Tee got out of the hospital and then she was gone.

"Bae I really don't know that yet but be home by eight tonight and I will have all that info for you." Jay said as he hugged her extra tight. He had to go before he started to cry. "I love you bae, I will call you tonight. I got to go. Wait for my call." Jay said as he walked away from her into the jailhouse doors.

Diamond had to sit in her car for a minute to get it together. It felt good to be free but now she felt empty because she still didn't know if the man that she loved was

Diary of a Triflin' Bitch

going to pull through this. Diamond made her way towards the hospital she had to see Tee Tee.

Diary of a Triflin' Bitch

Chapter 18

Terry

    Terry was sitting in the warehouse waiting on his goon to bring his money. Shit was getting crazy in the hood and Tip was blowing his phone up leaving message after message. The last message he listened to said something about her sister being kidnapped. He knew he had to go home and see what the hell that was about. That damn Brandy was always getting herself in trouble and calling Tip for help. First Jay got shot now the block was hot with cops, Dayshawn wasn't answering his phone and now Jay had turned himself in to go do his time. Terry really didn't know what to do about Jay. This nigga was really pissing him off. Maybe it was time to off that nigga and find somebody else to take his spot. Terry still didn't know what the nigga was locked up for, but he was soon to find out. He had already put a call in to the chick at the jailhouse in booking.

    "Aye yo that nigga Duke said he is on his way with that bread." Terry's right hand man said to him as he came

Diary of a Triflin' Bitch

from the backroom. They had been sitting there waiting on that nigga for over an hour.

"Alright let them other niggas know to be on alert. You can't ever be too careful in this game." Terry trusted nobody, not even his mother. That bitch moved the wrong way she would be dead too. After killing his daddy for beating his mother, he later found out that his mother was smoking crack and had stolen the rent money to get high and that's why his daddy was beating her ass. She also owed another dope boy some money for some crack she had credit. They came and kicked in the door while he was in school. After his father's death, he had to go into foster care because his mother couldn't take care of him and his sister. At the tender age of nine his mother was tricking his sister out to all the dope boys in the neighborhood for crack. Nobody but he and Tip knew this. He often thought about his sister; after he went into foster care they split them up, and he didn't know where she was.

"Alright man I got you." Trees said before he walked away. He knew his boss was in deep thought. He often got that way but Trees knew not to ask him about it.

Diary of a Triflin' Bitch

He had made that mistake once before and almost lost his life behind a question. Now he just kept his mouth shut. Terry was about two sandwiches short from a two person picnic. Trees wanted no parts of him. He just did as he was told and followed all the rules.

"Aye Trees after we get this money I need you to go to the jail and talk to Trudy and see why that nigga Jay was booked in today." Terry said. "And then get in contact with that nigga Dayshawn and call a meeting. That nigga haven't been answering his phone for me. If this info you get on Jay isn't good we might have to off these niggas." Terry said as he turned his head. That let Trees know the conversation was over so he walked away to go make those phone calls. He tried to stay on top of his game because he loved his life.

Terry went back to thinking of his childhood; he remembered he often had to make dinner for him and his sister. His father worked nights and his mother would leave them in the house alone all night long. Every month on the third his mother would go and sell all of their food stamps and spend her welfare check on crack. By the sixth of the

Diary of a Triflin' Bitch

month they had no food or money. He and his sister would have to go to the corner store and try to steal them something to eat. The store clerk caught on to what they were doing and kicked them out the store every time they would come in. After they were kicked out the store, a couple of times Terry had to come up with another way to feed them. His next step was to steal food from school. He would empty out his backpack before school and stack up on food he would steal throughout the day. He had watched the cafeteria ladies every day until he learned their routine. He knew when they all took their lunch, when they had a meeting to go to, or when they just took their breaks. Terry had their schedule down so good he would have two backpacks full of frozen dinners for him and his sister to eat.

"Aye Terry man you don't hear me calling you?" Trees asked for the third time. He had been calling Terry's name for the past five minutes. Terry was in the zone.

Terry snapped out of his zone and looked at Trees, "Man what the fuck do you want?" Terry asked out of frustration. His mind was on his sister real heavy lately.

Diary of a Triflin' Bitch

"Sorry to interrupt you man but Duke's ETA is about ten minutes now." Trees said with caution.

"Alright man thanks for letting me know and sorry for yelling at you." Terry knew he was out of place for yelling at Trees.

Terry walked to the back of the warehouse to wait on Duke to walk through the door. He could never be too sure about anything, so he was never in eye shot of anybody walking through the door of the warehouse. Terry heard the warehouse doors open, he waited until he heard it close and then he counted to sixty. This was something he always did because if anything was going to go down it would have happened in the first minute of the door opening. Terry walked out the backroom with his gun in hand, "My nigga what the hell took you so long to get here with my bread?" Asked Terry; with his gun pointing at Duke's head. He was ready to pull the trigger if this nigga's answer wasn't what he wanted to hear.

"Aye Terry you got it all wrong man, I ran into your chick on my way in. She was trying to get me to tell her where you were but I told her I didn't know." Duke said nervously. He also knew how trigger happy Terry could be.

Terry looked at Trees who walked over to Duke and snatched open his shirt, they had to make sure he didn't have on any wires. Duke's chest was bare he had no wires on him, but he knew he was still in trouble for being late.

Terry pulled his trigger and shot Duke in the left foot POW... Duke screamed out in agony, "Fuck man!" Duke screamed.

"That's for being late." Terry said and then shot him in his other foot...POW. "And that's for stopping with my mother fucking money on you!" Terry screamed in his face. He was pissed off. What if somebody was following him and had robbed him with Terry's money on him. "Your ass has been demoted. Bud you are now taking his place. Do you have a problem with that? Speak now or forever hold your peace." Terry said looking at Bud, who now had a look of horror on his face.

Diary of a Triflin' Bitch

"Nawl my dude thanks for the promotion. I can handle it." Bud said excited. He was happy and scared all at once.

"Now that we got this out the way, get this nigga up out of here. Does anybody else have a problem with being on time?" asked Terry as he looked around the room at the remaining niggas standing around. He didn't care if that nigga had stopped to talk to Jesus himself time was money.

"Ok Bud, Trees will get with you and show you the route you will have to take; you will learn it three different ways. Do not take the same route every day. If anything and I do mean anything happen to my money you will die. Do I make myself clear?" He asked looking Bud straight in the eyes.

"Nawl man I can handle it." Was all Bud could say. He knew he had just bitten off more than he could chew, but he needed the promotion bad.

"Ok Brick and Bud go count that up and let me know how much I got." Terry told them. He then said,

Diary of a Triflin' Bitch

"This meeting is over. Trees let me holla at you for a minute and the rest of you niggas clean up this mess and get the fuck out of here." Terry said and walked away.

"What's up boss what can I do for you?" Trees asked as he walked up to Terry.

"Did you get a chance to check on that for me yet?" Terry asked as he leaned up against the wall. He was real anxious about getting the info on Jay.

"Yeah man I talked to her that nigga has been booked for conspiracy to distribute heroin, possession of heroin and fleeing and eluding. She said they sentenced him to a year and a day." Trees felt good he already had that info on deck so quick. "I already put three calls out to that nigga Dayshawn but his phone is still going to voicemail. I am going by his house when I leave here." Trees kept talking.

"Good, good. Find out who we got on the inside cause that nigga Jay has to go. Get back with me today on this. I got to go home and see what the hell Tip got

Diary of a Triflin' Bitch

running." Terry said and walked away. He had to go check on her she was still calling non-stop.

Diary of a Triflin' Bitch

Chapter 19

Mad Black Woman

When Dayshawn woke up, he was in a very dark room. He couldn't remember what happened or where he was. He tried to look around the room, but he couldn't move anything but his head. Dayshawn heard water dripping but couldn't see anything. His head was pounding and his arms were taped above his head. He felt a draft in the room and that's when he realized he was completely naked. Now he was scared he had never been in a situation like this before. He was trying to think of who would want to harm him. But his mind kept coming up blank. Dayshawn heard a door open but the only thing he could see is a shadow of someone's body, he couldn't make out the face. The shadow walked closer in the room, and he now knew who it was.

"I see you're awake now. I thought I had killed you already when I laced your food with the LSD. Now the games can begin." Tracy said as she walked up in Dayshawn's face. It took her over an hour to drag his body

Diary of a Triflin' Bitch

down the stairs in the basement and get him taped up the way she wanted.

"Bae why, what are you doing? What the hell is going on here?" Asked Dayshawn he really didn't know what to think. Had Tracy gone mad?

"Well for starters let's have a little chat. When did you and that bitch Brandy start sleeping together?" Tracy asked getting straight to the point. She was pissed and hurt all at the same time.

"Huh, where did that come from?" asked Dayshawn. He wanted to know how much she really knew about him and Brandy.

This made Tracy angry so she walked over to her table of tricks and grabbed her whip. She walked back over to Dayshawn and brought her whip down across his back as hard as she could.

Dayshawn screamed out in pain, "AWW! What the hell are you doing?" and bucked against his restraints.

Diary of a Triflin' Bitch

This made Tracy smile so she hit him again and again. Dayshawn was making so much noise she had to stop and put tape across his mouth. Tracy continued to beat Dayshawn with her whip for another ten minutes. She had the strength of a bull and loved the pain she was putting him in. Tracy stopped to get her a drink of water. She had the cotton mouth from the coke and the LSD pill she took earlier.

"Now I'm going to remove the tape from your mouth and when I do I want you to tell me the truth or else it will be more pain for you." Tracy said before she removed the tape, "Now when the hell did you and Brandy start sleeping together?" Tracy asked again.

"I never slept with your girl bae I promise." Dayshawn was planning on lying to the end. He just couldn't make himself tell the truth. He knew he had gotten his self in some deep trouble and needed a way out.

Tracy put the tape back over his mouth, "Nope wrong answer!" Tracy said as she walked back over to her table of tricks, but this time she grabbed the spray bottle of

Diary of a Triflin' Bitch

ammonia. She had pain in her heart. How could two people she was so close to betray her like this? But it was ok she had Dayshawn's ass and Brandy would be next. She walked up less than a foot away from him and she started spraying Dayshawn in every wound on his body she had made with her whip. By the time she got to the front of his body he had passed out from the pain. Tracy slapped him around a couple of times while screaming at him.

"Wake your punk ass up nigga! I'm not done with you yet! You pussy ass nigga get up!" She screamed at him as she slapped him across the face.

Dayshawn woke up sweating from head to toe. He didn't know what had happened. He started looking around trying to find out where the hell he was at. When he saw Tracy standing in the corner smoking a cigarette, he remembered. Oh shit this bitch is gonna kill me. Dayshawn thought.

"Okay, I'm going to ask your ass one more time and I better get the answer I'm looking for or you will start losing fingers and toes." Laughed Tracy. What the fuck did

Diary of a Triflin' Bitch

she just say? Did she just say fingers and toes? Somebody please come save me from this crazy bitch! "Now for the last time tonight, HOW LONG HAVE YOU AND BRANDY BEEN SLEEPING TOGETHER?" She screamed in his face. Tracy was becoming very impatient with this asshole.

"Okay I will tell you everything, just please stop spraying me with that shit." Dayshawn asked with tears in his eyes his skin was on fire from the ammonia spray bath. "We started messing around about five years ago, but bae I tried to stop it, but she kept coming around. I'm sorry bae I know I was wrong for what I did but I do love you." He tried to plead his case.

"FIVE years ago, really nigga and you call that love? You fucking my cousin!" Tracy couldn't take it anymore she sprayed him in the eyes with the ammonia. That was most of their relationship, she had been faithful to his ass and this was the thanks she got. Tracy blacked out as she sprayed the remaining ammonia all over his body. When Tracy finished her bottle she threw it down on the ground. She grabbed her ice pick and with all of her might, she jammed the ice pick in his knee cap.

"OHHHH SHIT! OH MY GODDD! AWWWW!" Dayshawn woke up and screamed out in agonizing pain. His life started to flash before his eyes. He knew at that moment he was going to die. He never thought he would be killed at the hands of the woman he loved. Now he really knew what the older people meant when they said *"Hell knows no fury like a woman scorned."*

"Shut the fuck up you bitch made ass fuck nigga. You weren't doing all that crying when you were out there sucking, fucking and cheating on me. Now were you?" Tracy asked as she picked up her blade. She walked back over to Dayshawn very slowly. "Now I got one more question for you, if you tell me the truth I will not kill you. Do you got that?" Asked Tracy she needed to know where the hell Brandy was at. This question she wasn't sure Dayshawn knew the answer to. "Where the hell is Brandy at? She hasn't been answering her phone, and I know you have talked to her." Tracy said as she walked around him,

Diary of a Triflin' Bitch

Dayshawn was getting more and more nervous by the minute.

"She and Ant are down in Miami somewhere, I don't know where she is supposed to call me or text me when she gets an address to where they will be staying." Dayshawn said as fast as he could get it out. He was in so much pain.

"Miami huh? So that's where the bitch has been hiding at." Tracy said with a smile as she looked him in the eyes. She was tired of him crying and shit so she had something real sweet for his ass. First, Tracy cut out Dayshawn's tongue so he couldn't scream again, then she dropped down and relieved him of his third leg. Even though his tongue was gone, Dayshawn let out a scream from the pits of his soul. After he screamed out in pain he passed out again from the site of his own dick on the ground. Tracy said fuck it and proceeded to beat him where ever her bat could go. She swung her bat hard and kept beating him until he was dead. The shock from the pain was too intense for him so the last time he passed out his heart stopped. Tracy kept on beating him with her bat until

Diary of a Triflin' Bitch

she realized he wasn't moving. Tracy stood back to look at her handy work, she really put something on his ass. The last thing on her list to do to him was to cut him down; he had enough blood on the floor around him. She had some big sewer rats over in the corner.

Tracy cut Dayshawn body's down and it hit the ground with a big thud. Head first. She walked over to the cage where she had the rats, and opened it. The rats crawled around for about five minutes and then they smell the blood on the floor as Tracy turned and walked away the rats started feasting on Dayshawn's dead body. She grabbed all of her tools she had touched and put them in her bag where they belong. Then she stood there and watched the rats for a little while she was satisfied with the work she put in, so she just walked out of the basement.

When Tracy walked back up the stairs, it was as if a weight had been lifted off of her. She went in the living room and turned on the stereo system and before she knew it, she was dancing and cleaning up Dayshawn's house she didn't want it to be anything there that could link his death back to her. After cleaning up every room in the house that

Diary of a Triflin' Bitch

she had been in she emptied out his safe, grabbed her clothes out the closet, and turned off the lights. Tracy walked out of Dayshawn's house she left the stereo playing soft music and the front door cracked. When she got into her car a smile came across her face she was happy that chapter of her life was over. Now it was on to the next one.

Chapter 20

Akeem

Akeem was standing outside of the bathroom when Brandy came out; he looked at his watch she was a minute late. He slapped the shit out of her. He had to make sure she was on time for every job he sent her on. Brandy grabbed her face she knew it would be swollen in the morning. The only thing Akeem said to her was "follow me" and he kept walking toward the VIP rooms he wanted some much needed privacy. He walked right out the back door and got into the back of his truck. Brandy closed the door behind her.

"Did you take your panties off like I told you to?" Akeem said as he turned the light on in the truck.

"Yes I did." Brandy said with a little too much attitude. She found her head up against the window, and her arm twisted behind her back. "AWW!" Brandy screamed out in pain.

Diary of a Triflin' Bitch

"Let me make myself very clear when I ask you a question you will address me as daddy. You got that?" He asked; Brandy just shook her head up and down. Akeem twisted more on her arm, "AWW, please stop I'm sorry." Brandy said sounding like she was out of breath. The pain was so intense she was about to pass out. At that moment, she would do whatever it took for him to stop hurting her. She had never in her life been treated like this. She hated Ant for selling her to this lunatic.

"Address me as daddy! And I'm not going to tell you again. " Akeem said while putting pressure on her twisted arm.

"Yes daddy. Okay daddy. Anything you say daddy." Brandy made sure she stressed the word daddy. She just wanted the pain to stop.

"Now let's try this again did you take your panties off like I told you to?" Akeem asked again

"Yes daddy I did." Brandy said with the quickness. She was learning the rules fast. Now she knew this wasn't a

Diary of a Triflin' Bitch

game and if she wanted to survive this she had to do what she was told.

"Good now stand up and take the rest of your clothes off. I need to take a good look at my investment." Akeem said with a calm look on his face. She was more confused now more than ever; this man just went from yelling and twisting her arm to this nice calm man. "What the fuck?"

Brandy stood up so quick she hit her head on the roof of the truck, but she didn't care about that pain she knew first hand if she didn't do as he told her to there was going to be a different kind of pain. Brandy dropped all of her clothes to the floor of the truck; when she was completely naked she just stood there looking at Akeem.

"Wow Ant told me you had a beautiful body but damn! Man you were worth that million I paid that nigga." Akeem said pulling on his dick. His shit felt like it was going to break off in his pants. That statement made Brandy remember how she got there; that damn Ant was going to pay if it was the last thing on earth she did. "Now

Diary of a Triflin' Bitch

turn your fine ass around and let me see you from the back." He said getting more excited from the site of her apple bottom ass. This bitch got the body of a goddess. Man if her pussy is as good as her body looks I'm going to make a killing off her ass. Akeem thought to himself.

"Now bend over the seat and spread your legs open, let daddy smell you." He was really enjoying this; his dick was as hard as a brick. Fuck smelling this bitch I wanna taste her. Shit had just got real he hadn't met a bitch that could turn him on just by dropping her clothes in front of him in a long time.

Brandy did as she was told to do; she felt so dirty but she tried to play her role like a good girl. "Like this daddy. This how you want me? You like what you see daddy." Brandy said as she bent all the way over the seat and spread her legs as wide as she could. She even put an arch in her back so he could get a good look at her well shave pussy from the back.

Akeem almost busted a nut in his pants after seeing her pretty pink pearl sticking out between her lips. He knew

Diary of a Triflin' Bitch

she had to taste good with a pearl like that; he just had to taste her. He unzipped his pants to let his twelve inch monster out. That was another reason he had her to turn around he didn't want her to see how big his dick was. All the females he dealt with would see his dick and get scared. "Yes baby girl just like that. OMG! That is the most beautiful site I seen in a long time." He said massaging his dick. He rolled the condom down on his dick as far as it would go. He could never find a condom that fit his dick all the way.

"That pussy pretty ain't it daddy and she wet just for you." Brandy said playing with herself trying to entice him a little more. She liked to talk dirty to the men she dealt with; she thought this would make Akeem like her more and maybe not hit her anymore. "Come on and…" that was it Akeem had sucked on her clit so hard her voice got stuck in her throat. He was switching between sucking and blowing on her clit. Akeem grabbed both of her ass cheeks and spread them open wider to taste her sweet nectar she tasted so sweet to him. Brandy was feeling nasty at first, but the way Akeem was sucking and blowing on her clit had her getting weak in the knees. She had never had a man

Diary of a Triflin' Bitch

to take control over her body and suck on her clit with that much experience.

"Damn baby you taste so good. Whose pussy is this?" Akeem said while spreading her pussy lips open. "Cum for daddy. I want to see you cum. Can you cum for daddy?" He said right before he dove back in her wetness. Brandy didn't know it but she had Akeem under her spell. The way her pussy smelled and tasted had him open like the Waffle House. Her pussy juices had that nigga gone already, and he hadn't even felt the pussy.

"Oooh shit daddy right there; eat your pussy daddy. This is your pussy daddy. OMG! Don't move daddy I'm about to cum daddy! Shit daddy can I please cum in your mouth daddy?" Brandy asked she was on the verge of exploding if he kept sucking her clit like that, but she was afraid to cum in his mouth before he gave her the okay.

"Hell yeah let daddy see how your pussy juices taste!" Akeem said as he licked her asshole right before he stuck his finger in it. Brandy arched her back from the pain of his finger in her asshole; she had never had anything in

Diary of a Triflin' Bitch

her asshole before this. It was truly a first for her, after Akeem started sucking on her clit again and finger fucking her asshole the pain went away, and she started to enjoy it. Before she knew it, he had her bent over so far she was looking at him through her legs. He didn't know she was that flexible. Shit was feeling so good to her she spread her own ass cheeks so he could have easy access to both of her holes.

"Here it comes daddy I'm about to cum. OMG! Suck your pussssy!" Brandy yelled before she exploded in his mouth. Her pussy juices went all over Akeem's face and down his chin; they were so good he forgot who and what she was. Akeem sucked her until she was dry. He got every last drop. Damn she tastes better than Emily I might have to hit this on the regular. He thought to himself as he sat back in the seat. Brandy was so spent she couldn't even stand up straight. That was one of the best and longest nuts she had ever had.

"Now come sit down in daddy lap and let me feel you." Akeem said wiping his face with the back of his hands. It was time to give her the meat. He knew once she

Diary of a Triflin' Bitch

saw or felt it he was going to have to force her to take the dick. Brandy had different plans for him. She turned around and got down on her knees. She started to crawl over to him; it was so dark in the truck she couldn't see where she was going. She only heard his breathing, so she followed it. When she reached him, she reached up and grabbed his dick and almost fainted. She had never in her life seen or felt a dick this size before. She soon regretted wanting to please him orally.

Akeem felt her hesitation and spoke up, "Nawl baby girl this what you wanted so take this dick for daddy." He said as he grabbed the back of her neck and guided her to his dick. Brandy took a deep breath and opened her mouth as wide as she could get it. She knew she couldn't back down now. As she began sucking on the head of his dick, she felt it grow. She knew she had to relax, or it was going to be a long painful night. As she relaxed a little bit she got into it more. Before she knew it her pussy was wet again, and she was playing with herself. Brandy had about nine inches of his dick down her throat and loved it. Akeem was in heaven; this bitch had nine inches of him down her

Diary of a Triflin' Bitch

throat and wasn't gagging. He tried to get another two inches down there but Brandy started to choke.

"Damn baby girl I hope your pussy is as good as your face. I know now I got to keep you on my team. Come fuck daddy, and you better not scream." Akeem said as he pulled Brandy up by her hair; when he had her in the position he wanted her in he forced the first five inches in her pussy.

Brandy yelp out in pain, "not so fast daddy. Please take it easy." Brandy said trying to catch her breath. If this man didn't take it easy, he was going to rip her a new asshole. She had to try and position herself so the pain would go away. She didn't have much room in the back of the truck so she just pressed her body up against his as hard as she could to get leverage. Akeem started to move nice and slow for her he was trying to find out just how much dick she could really take. Brandy started to get into it also, and her pain turned into pleasure. She started riding him like the cowgirl she thought she was.

Diary of a Triflin' Bitch

Once Brandy found her rhythm she started to contract her pussy muscles and fucked the hell out of Akeem. His pogo stick was one of the best she'd had and she was having the time of her life. Brandy even turned around and rode his dick from the back. He couldn't take the power of her pussy any longer, he busted an elephant sized nut. Both of them were spent from their hour long fuck session so all you heard was breathing in the truck.

Diary of a Triflin' Bitch

Chapter 21

Diamond

On Diamond's way back home from the jail she called Dayshawn twice but still didn't get an answer. She really needed to get in contact with him about that money. She even gave Tracy a call shit had been so crazy in the last week she hadn't had a chance to talk to her friend. *"Hey girl, when you get out the bed with that nigga give me a call. Yeah Jay told me you two were back together. Y'all musta had a long night because neither one of y'all are answering the phone. Call me back I need to holla at you about something important. And oh yeah tell Dayshawn I need to chat with him too. Love you bye."* Diamond hung up her phone she would call Tracy back after she left the hospital, she was going to see Tee Tee.

"Hey, Ms. Wise I see you have become very close to the patient in room 222. You even come here on your days off just to check on him." stated Adam, her coworker. Diamond didn't like his garbage mouth ass. His breath

Diary of a Triflin' Bitch

always turned her stomach. And he was always trying to flirt with her.

"Yeah, I guess you're right Adam, he has kind of grown on me. His family doesn't know he is here, so he never has any visitors. How is he doing today? Has Dr. Lacy come in yet to see him?" Diamond asked trying to sound nonchalant about the situation. She really didn't need him all up in her business.

"Nawl not yet and he is doing okay. His fever is back and he still hasn't come out of his coma yet. Dr. Lacy's report states he has an infection somewhere so the tube will have to stay in until they get that under control. Your man doesn't mind you always coming up here checking on another man?" Adam was tired of playing these games with her. He was planning on blackmailing her for some ass. He had never met Jay before, but he knew of him.

"Excuse me." Diamond said caught off guard.

Diary of a Triflin' Bitch

"You heard me Ms. Wise. Does Jay know you be up here all the time seeing and taking care of another man. I mean you come here and bathe him, lotion him down, change his bedding and talking to him like you know him. It can be our little secret if you want it to but you have to grant me just one night with you." Adam said with a smile. He had put it out there now he had to see if she falls for the bait. He had been in love with Diamond ever since he first saw her.

"You son of a bitch! I don't think that is any of your business. And how the hell do you know Jay?" Diamond asked with fire in her eyes. She was pissed she had to find out more to see how much he knew. She had never seen him around Jay's people before or even heard Jay mention his name.

"Now that I got your attention let's just say a good friend of mines is Jay's right hand man. How do you think I got this job working so closely with you? Yeah they placed me here just to watch you. Now you wouldn't want Jay to find this out would you?" Adam asked her, watching her every movement. He could tell she was getting nervous and he loved to see her sweat.

"You got to be fucking kidding me. I thought you were my friend; how could you do me like this? And you have been spying on me?" Diamond was shocked at how far Jay's reach was. Out of all of the years of knowing him she never realized the level of power Jay had. She would have never thought of him placing somebody at her job to keep tabs on her.

"I know Jay had to go turn his self in this morning so now I'm supposed to report back to Dayshawn. Now about me being your friend you never gave me the chance to. You always had your nose stuck up at a brother. And baby girl I wouldn't call it spying it is just another one of my many jobs I get paid for. Now I know you would love this one so listen closely." Adam said before he took a recorder of his work shirt. When he pushed play tears ran down Diamond's face, "Tee Tee, please pull through this bae. Our unborn child is depending on you. I can't do this by myself. You told me that if I left Jay we could be together. Boo who did this to you? Wake up and tell me

Diary of a Triflin' Bitch

who put you in here. I love you." Diamond couldn't breathe. Her world as she knew it had stopped.

"Now you see I do all of my jobs very well. You are kind of messy for this one you are having a baby by your man's friend. Man if one of Jay's workers can get some play then I know I damn sure can. So when are you going to let me have you for one night. You have dinner with me and spend the night with me I will destroy this here tape. My job is coming to an end in about three days, so you pick a day and time." Adam said with much confidence.

"So if I don't go out with you and sleep with you, you are going to blackmail me? Are you serious! Now you are doing the most. Man, fuck you and that damn tape. You will never have a chance in hell with me stank mouth ass nigga." Diamond screamed a little bit too loud. Another coworker passing by started to stare at them. This nigga really got me fucked up! Diamond thought to herself.

Adam got up from out of his chair he had been sitting in and walked closer to Diamond. Because what he was about to say, he didn't want or need anybody else to

Diary of a Triflin' Bitch

hear. Through clench teeth and in a calm demeanor Adam spoke, "I may have the stank mouth, so you say but know this here, I am to turn this tape and the rest of my info in to Dayshawn in three days and once he gets it if he finds something incriminating anywhere in this here info he already has orders to kill you. So you now have a decision to make one night with me or you go swimming with the fish." Adam said and smiled at her.

This bastard! He must not know who the hell he playing with. Okay, he wants me to spend one night with him; I got him it's going to be his last night on this here earth. Lights out for this dick head! Diamond was standing there thinking to herself. "Okay, damn I will spend one night with you but you have to promise to give me that damn tape and all the info you got. And for the record I just want you to know you are a sorry no good ass nigga for what you are making me do and you know I'm pregnant. I know you already have my number so call me in two days and we can set it up for then." Diamond said and started walking away madder than a bitch. Adam was making her sick and dizzy just thinking about sleeping with him.

Diary of a Triflin' Bitch

"They say pregnant pussy is the best pussy!" Adam said right before she got out of earshot. That pussy is going to be good. That bitch walk like she got good pussy! Adam thought to himself as he walked away to go do the rest of his work before his shift was over.

Diary of a Triflin' Bitch

Chapter 22

Tip

Tip had been riding around for the last five hours looking for Terry; his ass hadn't been answering his phone all damn day. She was in straight panic mode about her sister and didn't know where to go or what to do. Tip didn't realize it until it was too late that she needed some gas. Her car turned off and she coasted it over to the side of the road. Shit! Now what the fuck am I going to do now? Nobody is answering their phone. Damn it this is all Terry's fault. She thought to herself. She had to blame somebody other than herself.

Tip hit the steering wheel out of frustration. Today felt like a day from hell. First Akeem calls and demands she either set Terry up for his loot or he was going to come get her, then he also informs her that he is holding her sister hostage until it happens. She pulled her phone from her purse and tried to call Terry again; she got his damn voicemail again. *"Terry when you get this message please call me back. My damn car has run out of gas, and now I'm*

Diary of a Triflin' Bitch

on the side of the road." She hung up the phone and kept going through her call log at that moment she didn't care who came to get her off the side of the road.

It hit her like a light bulb, "Diamond" she hurried up and called Diamond. When Diamond answered her phone Tip started talking nonstop, "Thank GOD you answered I really need for you to come bring me some gas. Girl shit is crazy and I've been driving around all damn day looking for Terry's ass and done ran out of gas. It seems like everybody I call not answering their phone." Tip said all in one breath.

"Tip calm down girl you don't need to be stressing yourself out. You are pregnant just tell me where you are so I can come." Diamond said out of breath. She was just leaving the hospital and not feeling good at all.

"Diamond are you okay? You don't sound too good. What's wrong?" Tip asked turning her stress level down some but now she was worried more about her friend.

Diary of a Triflin' Bitch

"No, I'm not okay but when I get to where you are we will talk about it. You know I can't say much over the phone. Now where are you?" Diamond said sitting in her car waiting on the directions. She was just glad she was going to be able to get some shit off her chest. She knew whatever she told Tip would not get repeated.

"Ok, I'm down east by the park. You will see me after you pass the damn gas station. I will be on your right hand side of the road about a mile past it." Tip said and, laughed all at once because the shit was so funny.

"I'm on my way, please stay in the car and lock the doors. It's too dark outside, and you know they be robbing and shooting people down east." Diamond said with concern in her voice. You wouldn't dare catch her down east after dark. The niggas down east don't give a fuck about the code of the streets, they will kill women and kids at the drop of a dime.

"Girl you don't have to tell me twice, my doors are already locked and the windows are up. Hell I don't even have on my hazard lights. Hurry up you done got me scared now." Tip said making sure her doors were locked for real.

"Ok I will be there as fast as I can. I still got to stop to the store and get some gas so give me about thirty minutes. I'm coming hang tight." Diamond said before she ended the call she was truly on a mission. She had to get to Tip quick.

Tip tried to keep herself busy while she waited for Diamond. She felt a little better now that she had gotten in touch with some damn body. Her day was pretty fucked up and she just wanted to get home take a bath and go to sleep. She would just have to deal with the Brandy situation tomorrow. Tip picked up her phone to give Terry a call to let him know to disregard her last message she would be home in less than an hour.

Terry's phone was now ringing so that mean he had turned it back on. Tip smiled because she really needed to talk to him. Please answer the phone bae. Tip thought trying to will him to do so. "Where the hell are you at?"

Diary of a Triflin' Bitch

Terry yelled as soon as he answered his phone. He was pissed she hadn't made it home yet.

"Bae I was out looking for you because you weren't answering your phone. Have you spoken to Duke?" Tip asked feeling like a child being chastised.

"Nawl was I supposed to talk to him? And you still haven't told me where you are." Terry lied to see what she was going to say. He had to make sure her story was going to be the same as Duke's or he would kill Duke for lying.

"I saw Duke earlier at the red light and asked him where you were. He told me he didn't know and pulled off when the light turned green. So I drove down east to see if I saw your car at your mother's house and ran out of gas. Now I'm sitting on the side of the road waiting for Diamond to come bring me some gas so I can come home." Tip said taking a deep breath. She knew if Terry got too mad at her he would beat her ass. Their relationship was never like that in the beginning. Terry was the kindest and gentlest man she had ever met.

Diary of a Triflin' Bitch

"Down east? Looking for me? Ran out of gas? On the side of the road? Man what the fuck you got running today? Now you know my mother don't stay down east no more, so you had no business going down there. Lie to me again about why you are down east, and I'm going to put my foot up your ass." Terry said now heading down east he didn't want anything to happen to her down there.

"Bae can we please talk about this when I get home you know I can't say too much over the phone. Shit is crazy right now, but I was looking for somebody that may know where or who took my sister." Tip said in tears. It had just hit her that she may not see her sister alive ever again.

"We are going to talk about this when I get there. Sit your ass in that car and don't move. I will be there in ten minutes. Do you hear me?" Terry said pushing the gas pedal a little harder.

"Yes bae I hear you. I think I see Diamond's car pulling up behind me so I will have her to sit with me until

Diary of a Triflin' Bitch

you get here." Tip said as she was unlocking her car doors getting out the car.

"Tip are you sure that's Diamond behind you..." The phone went blank. Terry looked at his phone and saw the call had dropped, so he called her back and got no answer. This scared the hell out of him. He called back again and again until the last time he called and her phone went straight to voicemail *"You have reached Tip leave it at the beep! If not I will holla at you! BEEP."* Terry's heart dropped in the pit of his stomach he knew then something was really wrong.

Diary of a Triflin' Bitch

Chapter 23

Tracy

Father can you hear me, I need your love today. I know that you are listening; you hear men every day. Father please hear us; And we will be ok… Tracy's phone kept playing her favorite gospel song indicating it was ringing. She had fallen asleep in her hotel room that she had gotten after she killed Dayshawn. The coke had her too paranoid to go home she thought for sure Dayshawn's goons were coming to kill her. Tracy looked down at her phone she noticed she had fifteen missed calls and five voice messages. Tracy still had murder on her mind; now that she had slept off her high. She needed to find out where Ant and Brandy were at in Miami. I know who might know where Brandy's ass is. I need to call Tip's ass to see how much she knows about Brandy being gone. But damn I just can't let her know that I'm going to kill her sister because that would be another witness. I don't need anybody to know about these murders. Tracy thought to herself as she was making her way into the bathroom.

Diary of a Triflin' Bitch

"Housekeeping!" Tracy heard someone say as they were banging on the door before she reached the bathroom door.

"How can I help you?" Tracy yelled back she was scared to open the door.

"Ma'am its check out time; are you staying or leaving?" The housekeeper said. She was trying to get all of her rooms done early so she could go home.

"I'm leaving give me fifteen minutes and I will be out of here." Tracy said as she walked back to the bathroom to get a quick shower so she could get the hell out of there.

Tracy was showered, packed, and in her car in no time. She wasn't feeling too safe in that room. First place she went was to McDonald's for something to eat. She was hungry as hell. After she had ordered her food, she parked her car in the parking lot so she could eat and make a couple of phone calls. Tracy called Tip first; she really needed to talk to her to see if she knew where Brandy was. She called Tip twice and got her voicemail both times so

Diary of a Triflin' Bitch

she left her a message, *"Aye hoe call me back looks like we are playing phone tag with each other. I know I been off the scene for a minute, but I need to talk to you about something. So when you get a chance call me back. Love you."*

Tracy hung up her phone and shook her head at the thought of her having to kill one of her family members. But the bitch had to go, cousin or not. She listened to all of her voice mails before she made another call. She was glad too because she was going to call Diamond back, but not after she heard Diamond's voicemail, *"Hey girl when you get out the bed with that nigga give me a call. Yeah Jay told me you two are back together. Y'all musta had a long night because neither one of y'all ain't answering the phone. Call me back I need to holla at you about something important. And oh yeah tell Dayshawn I need to chat with him to. Love you bye."* Tracy replayed the message before she deleted it. She couldn't call Diamond back because she might ask where Dayshawn was at and Tracy still hadn't come up with the excuse to tell people about why he was MIA. She didn't know if anybody had found his remains yet, so she was not about to start answering questions just yet.

Diary of a Triflin' Bitch

Tracy listened to her next voicemail and shook her head. It was from Ms. Lisa Adams the lady from the clinic. She really didn't want to be bothered by her right now she would just give her a call when she felt up to it. That was the end of her voice messages, so Tracy looked through her call log she just remembered she had fifteen missed calls. She saw out of them fifteen missed calls one number had called her eight times but she didn't recognize the number. Tracy said fuck it and called the number back. If it was somebody she didn't want to talk to she would just hang up.

"Damn baby girl you screening all your calls? This Bo Peep what's up?" He said turning his music down so he could hear her.

"Nawl boo I just was tied up for a minute and couldn't answer the phone. What you got running?" Tracy asked perking up she really was feeling him. Now that Dayshawn is out the picture she had to see what he was all about.

Diary of a Triflin' Bitch

"Shit I'm trying to see you, can you make that happen? I would like to finish our little conversation we were having and get to know you a little better." He said holding his breath waiting on her answer she was his only link he had for getting to Jay and Dayshawn.

"I think I would like that, but I got a couple of things to do first and then I will be free. Let's say we meet up about nine tonight? Is that cool with you?" She asked him with a smile on her face.

"Aye baby nine it is. How about you meet me at Joe's Toes about that time? You do eat seafood don't you?" He asked. He had just forgotten that quick that he didn't know too much about her.

"Seafood is one of my many favorites to eat I will be there and make sure you are on time. You know how y'all men do." She said with a laugh.

"Nawl baby girl I'm a grown ass man. I would never keep something as sexy as you waiting for nothing. You don't be late and bring that sexy ass body of yours to

Diary of a Triflin' Bitch

daddy." He said flirting back, but he wasn't lying she did have a sexy ass body.

"Thanks for the compliment and I will be there handsome. Talk to you then. Bye." She said before she hung up the phone. Tracy rushed the conversation because she was starting to feel like a school girl again, and his deep voice was making her wet. Hell if he played his cards right he just might get some.

Diary of a Triflin' Bitch

Chapter 24

Jay

Jay was walking the yard with one of his workers. He was trying to see how many of his nigga was in the county jail. He knew now that he had to do this time he needed to be clicked up in order to make it through this year.

"Aye Bre tell me how many niggas from our camp do we have up in here?" Jay asked.

"Man we got about ten niggas in this bitch. We been doing good making money up in here, but we do have some beef from some of those cats over there." Bre nodded his head in the direction he wanted Jay to look.

Jay looked over at the niggas on the weight bench before he spoke. "What you mean we got some beef with those niggas? Man we don't beef we kill then ask question later." Jay said with his voice laced with venom.

Diary of a Triflin' Bitch

"I know what you mean but see they started beefing with us because we took most of their profits. We got to three of their people, but they are still coming at us. That lil nigga sitting on the bench over there is the leader of their click. He is a hard nigga to touch." Bre said angrily. He had been trying to get at that nigga for the longest.

"Alright call a meeting for after chow. I told y'all lil niggas if you kill the head the body will die. We going to get at that nigga and the rest of his click will fall in line." Jay said now plotting on how he was going to pull it off.

"Alright boss I got you." Bre said and ran off to go spread the news. He was trying to become Jay's right hand man now that Dayshawn was on the outside, so he had to do a good job.

Jay walked the yard one more time scoping things out before he headed back in. It was hot as hell outside he needed a drink of water then he would go call Diamond to make sure she was ok and in the house safely. As Jay was drinking his water, he watched niggas all around him playing cards, dominos, chess, reading, and just talking

Diary of a Triflin' Bitch

shit. This was going to be a very long year for him. Jay walked away heading to the phones, when he saw the line was long he turned around and said to his self, I will just come back after I shower these niggas got all of the phones on lock. I got to get me a cell phone quick I forgot how these niggas be caking on the damn phones.

Jay went to his cell to gather his things for his shower after he had showered he would go see the C.O. about visiting hour, paying for protection, and getting him a cell phone. He knew it was going to cost him a grip but hell it was a small price to pay to keep in touch with the outside world whenever he wanted to and his life. Jay walked out of his cell headed to the showers but he was slipping. He never saw the young man standing over in the corner watching his every move.

Jay entered the shower and began to soap up his 6'2" toned body. At the age of 31-years-old he knew he had a great body. Out of nowhere he was attacked from behind. At first he was shocked that somebody was trying to get at him on his first day in but he was going to make a prime example out of whoever this was. The man had Jay

Diary of a Triflin' Bitch

in a head lock from behind trying to get his shank out of his pocket. Jay kept trying to push his self away from the wall. He knew if this nigga got him pinned up against the wall it would be over for him. Jay was able to push himself off the wall hard enough to get some leverage and stand up straight. He elbowed the man in the stomach and the man drop his shank on the shower floor. Jay then head butted the man who then released his neck. Jay got his second wind and went to work on the man's face. After a couple of combos to the man's face and body he fell to the floor of the shower room floor. Jay started raining blows to the man's face using his foot. The man balled up in a ball and wished the beating would be over soon. After Jay realized he was winning this fight he eased up on his beating, he had to find out who sent him.

"Who the fuck you work for nigga?" Jay said to the man as he kicked him in the head again and again. He stopped to give the man some time to answer him.

"Dude I'm sorry I thought you was somebody else." The man said out of breath. He lied to Jay because he didn't want to give up his boss's name.

Diary of a Triflin' Bitch

"Nawl my dude you came at the right nigga now who sent you at me? Lie to me again and I will cut your throat." Jay said as he picked up the shank off the floor he wanted to know who sent him. He didn't think he had no enemies but soon found out every man in the game had an enemy no matter what.

"Alright I will tell you man, just don't kill me. Man I got two kids on the outside. If I tell you, you got to protect me if they find out I told you anything they are gonna kill me. Let me in your camp please." The young man begged he was afraid to die.

"Alright nigga just tell me what I need to know before all of your guts are out here on the floor. Your ass will be shitting out of a bag for the rest of your life." Jay said raising the shank in the air. He was going to kill him anyway he knew he couldn't let this man live. If he let him live that would be another enemy after him. If this man had the balls to come after him this time, he would do it again.

"Ok man Terry Wilson sent me something about you being a dry snitch. You got ten stacks on your head."

Diary of a Triflin' Bitch

The young man said as he attempted to get up off the floor only to be kicked back down by Jay. When Jay heard his connect name come out of the young man's mouth, he snapped. He went back to work on the young man until he wasn't breathing. Jay walked out the shower room as if nothing had happened, mad and very confused. What the hell did the man mean by dry snitching? Jay just shook his head and went back to his cell. He had to come up with a way for him to get out of jail because if he stayed behind bars he was going to be a dead man.

Chapter 25

Brandy

Brandy was only in Miami for three days and already was the highest paid hoe in her camp. She came to grips with her new lifestyle and told herself that if she had to do it she was going to be the best at it. Today was moving day; she and five other girls would be placed in the house, two girls to a room. They all were newbie's, so they were called by the other girls. Brandy was ready to move into the house that way she would have more privacy to come up with her plan to escape. She had been sharing this one room with these girls, and it has been hell.

"Aye Pink Pearl is these yours?" yelled a dark skinned girl from the bathroom. All of the girls were trying to get their stuff together for the move.

"Nawl Hazel I think they belongs to Cherry but she not here she worked the night shift last night. Give it here I will put it in her bag." Brandy answered to her new street name. Akeem had given all the girls their street names. He

Diary of a Triflin' Bitch

chose their names by the way they looked or something on their bodies. The girl Brandy was talking to was called Hazel because of her hazel green eyes.

"I think this is hers also. I cleaned up the bathroom so there is nothing else left in there to do." Hazel said.

"What time did daddy say we had to be ready by again?" Asked Brandy, who had learned about her mouth and her tardiness.

"He told me we had to be out the room by nine." Hazel stated while she was placing bag after bag by the door. She was so ready for her to be in her own bed.

"Hell it's already 8:36 so we need to be making our way downstairs. These hoes are going to have to pay us for getting their stuff out this room." Brandy said as she grabbed two bags plus her own. Both girls walked out the room with three bags a piece heading for the elevators. When Brandy and Hazel made their way to the lobby two of the other newbie's were walking in smiling.

Diary of a Triflin' Bitch

"Damn girl thank you for getting my stuff for me I owe you one. I will do your house chores for a week. We are running a little late because Sticks had a problem with her last john." The white girl said to Brandy.

"Thanks Spots I was thinking more like clean my room but my house chores are cool. Sticks are you ok; that pussy didn't hurt you did he?" Brandy asked her before smiling at Spots.

"Yeah girl I'm cool do you have my bag too I need to freshen up before we leave up out of here." Sticks said.

"Nawl Hazel grabbed your bag I have Cherry's bag." Brandy told her the girl look tired from all of her late nights she was keeping trying to keep up with Brandy. Hazel looked up and saw the truck pull up, so she handed Sticks her bag and went to go get in the truck.

"Well, hurry up you know how daddy gets when we're late." Brandy said before she walked away and got in the truck. The other girls made it in the truck on time, so nobody got chastised or punished. The ride to the house

Diary of a Triflin' Bitch

was a short one. When they pulled up to the house Brandy noticed it was the same house Ant had tricked her into thinking was going to be hers.

"Pink Pearl are you ok?" Cherry whispered because she saw how Brandy's face color had changed.

"Hell Nawl I'm not alright but we will talk about this once we get into the house." Brandy whispered back she really didn't want anybody in her business but she had come to like Cherry as a friend and sexually. When the truck came to a stop in the driveway nobody moved. That was another one of their rules to not to speak or move unless you are told to do so.

"Ok ladies I was instructed to tell you all when you get into this house you are to line your bags up in the foyer; then have a seat in the dining room where the next meeting will be held." Their driver spoke to them with much respect and a dangerous look on his face. Nobody still moved out of their spots. "If you all understand what I just said you may get out the truck and proceed in the house." He said.

Diary of a Triflin' Bitch

That was their queue to move; so all the girls hopped out of the truck and grabbed their bags. Each girl was in awe with the site of this house but Brandy. With each step she took she became madder and madder. This house changed her life, and she wanted it back. She had thoughts of burning it down to the ground with whomever in it. As each girl was granted access to enter the house they did what was asked of them, by lining up their bags in the foyer then went and had a seat in the dining room. Nobody spoke for the next ten minutes until Akeem and Ant walked in the room from their breakfast meeting.

"Good morning ladies how are each one of y'all doing this morning?" Asked Akeem; looking at the woman sitting at this table. "Speak from left to right." He told them.

"Good morning daddy I am doing well this morning. My take from last night was $1937" Spots said with a smile on her face. She was proud of herself. She placed the money on the table in front of her. Akeem just shook his head up and down.

Diary of a Triflin' Bitch

"Good morning daddy my morning is well also. My take from last night is $1490." Sticks said and followed Spots lead.

"Morning daddy I'm blessed to be here this morning and my take from last night was $1502. Hazel said while placing her money on the table as well.

The other three ladies greeted him with the same greeting and did the same with their money. Blackie's take was $1350, Cherry's take was $2050, and Brandy's take was a grand total of $2700. Akeem was yet impressed again with the money Brandy was bringing in. All the girls were trying to figure out how she made so much money and she wasn't out with them all night.

"Oh now that we got that out of the way the top dollar award goes to Pink Pearl again. Ladies y'all need to step your game up and make me some more money. Pink Pearl since you have won the top dollar award for today your reward is a night off, you can pick your roommate out, and you get to pick which room you would like to sleep in." he said smiling at her. "Ladies we will do this every

Diary of a Triflin' Bitch

Sunday morning at nine now that you all have a home. The only thing won't change is your roommates, whoever you are bunking with become one because if one fucks up the other gets punished also. Do you all understand me" Akeem asked the girls.

"I pick Cherry as my roommate daddy." Brandy said quickly she knew if Cherry was her roommate they would win the top dollar reward every month.

"Now down to business let me introduce you all to Ant. He will be y'alls house mate. Whenever I'm not present what he tells you is gold. If he has any problems out of any of you he already has the orders to punish you. He will be running this house so he may have a couple of rules of his own that you will need to follow. Am I clear on this?" Akeem asked as he looked around the table at all of the girls. "That concludes my part of this meeting I will now turn it over to Ant you ladies have a great day off." With that being said, Akeem walked out of the dining room and left the house.

Diary of a Triflin' Bitch

All the girls except Brandy were excited about picking out their rooms and getting settled in. They had no problems with Ant they all thought he was fine as wine, so it was going to be easy for them to follow his rules. Brandy, on the other hand, had a look of disgust on her face as they were dismissed to their rooms. Ant saw it and made a mental note to have a personal meeting with her later on.

Diary of a Triflin' Bitch

Chapter 26

Diamond

Diamond had gotten that phone call from Adam and the day had come for them to go out. She wasn't in the mood to deal with him tonight, she hadn't heard from Tip in two days. When she did finally get to her car that night she wasn't there, it was like she had fallen off the face of the earth. Her phone was still going to voicemail and Terry said he was looking for her but she still hadn't heard from either one of them. Diamond finished applying her make up and took a long look in the mirror at herself. Diamond grabbed her purse and headed out the door to go to the address Adam had texted her earlier. When she got into her car, she made sure she had her gun in her purse. She was trying to make this quick so she could get back to her life, and find out what was happening to all of her friends. Brandy was MIA, Tracy hasn't returned any of her calls, and now Tip was missing. She and Tip's mother had filed a missing persons report, but the police weren't doing their jobs either.

Diary of a Triflin' Bitch

Diamond pulled up to the house Adam stayed in and cut off her engine to her car. She had put a stolen tag on her car earlier so if anybody saw or heard her leave, they would have the wrong tag number to give to the cops. As Diamond made her way to the door she was greeted by Adam. He had on a suit, he was clean shaved and smelling good. She was very surprised at how well he cleaned up.

"Hey beautiful, how are you tonight?" Adam asked as he was taking her coat. He was going to be the perfect gentlemen tonight maybe he could change Diamond's way of thinking about him.

"Not well my stomach is queasy do you have any ginger ale?" Diamond spoke truthfully.

"Why yes I do right this way." He said as he led her into the dining room. He had the table set up so nice for them. He pulled out her chair for her to sit down. "Would you like any ice to go with it?" He asked her.

"Yes please." Diamond was feeling so sick she didn't have time to be mean or nasty to him.

Diary of a Triflin' Bitch

Adam came back with the unopened ginger ale; he wanted her to know he wasn't trying to drug or poison her. He wanted to do nothing but take care of her for life. "Here you go." He said before sitting the ginger ale and the cup of ice down in front of her. "Can I get you anything else before I go check on our dinner?" He asked her out of concern this time she really wasn't looking too good.

"No, this will be fine. Thanks." She said to him before looking around the room. For the first time, she realized how nice it was in his house.

"Ok dinner will be ready in a minute. You can make yourself at home or you can come in the kitchen with me." Adam said intoxicated by her smell and beauty. He was in love with her and didn't know it.

"You mind if I go into your front room to look at TV for a while until you are through in there." Diamond asked she really needed to lay down the room was starting to spin on her.

Diary of a Triflin' Bitch

"Go ahead baby I will call you when our dinner is ready." He said to her as he tried to help her up out of her chair.

"I'm okay Adam go ahead and check on dinner I can make it in there by myself." She said with a smile it was really a different side of him she never saw before. She could get used to a man catering to her like this but too bad he had to die. Diamond made her way into the living room while Adam turned on his heels to go check on their dinner. His feelings were a little hurt by the way she just brushed him off.

By the time dinner was ready Diamond had dozed off to sleep. Adam stood and watched her sleep for a while he was so mesmerized by her beauty. He tapped her on her shoulder to wake her, "Diamond dinner is ready." He told her when she opened her eyes.

"I'm really not hungry sorry. But can I take my food to go?" She asked him with a smile.

Diary of a Triflin' Bitch

"Sure, I will go wrap it up for you then. I will come in here, and we can watch a movie before we go to bed." Adam said as he walked away and went back into the kitchen. He cleared the table and wrapped her food to go. After cutting off all the lights, he joined her in the living room. "Your food is in the microwave. So what movie would you like to watch?" He asked her as he made his way over to the DVD player.

"It really doesn't matter to me but if you got anything funny down there that would be cool." She said to him.

"Ok you can choose from Ride Along or Black Coffee." He said to her waiting on her pick.

"Let's see Ride Along. The previews are funny as hell." She said wrapping up in the cover a little tighter. Well at least I can watch a good movie and it won't be a wasted night. Diamond thought to herself.

Adam came and made himself comfortable next to her. They made small talk for the first forty-five minutes of

Diary of a Triflin' Bitch

the movie while Adam rubbed her feet. After a while the room grew quiet and they watched the movie. By the time the movie was over Diamond was sleep again. This time she had fallen asleep lying on her back with both of her feet on the couch. Adam saw this as his opportunity to taste her; he had waited long enough.

Adam eased her dress up above her waist and exposed he panties. She had on a pair of thongs. Instead of removing her panties all the way he just got down on one knee and pulled them to the side. Diamond's pussy was neatly shaved, and he loved the smell coming from down there. Adam pressed her pussy lips together to make her clit stick out a little further, and then he gently sucked on her clit in a circular motion. OMG! I knew she would taste good. He thought to his self as he sucked up her juices that were seeping out of her tunnel. Adam needed full access to the pussy he picked her leg up, the one that was almost about to fall off the couch and put it in the crook of his neck. That little gesture opened her pussy lips and the site he saw was hypnotizing. He dove back in this time with a little more pressure to her clit.

Diary of a Triflin' Bitch

Diamond must have been having a wet dream or dreaming about the next nigga because next thing Adam knew she had her hands on the back of his head guiding him to her spot. He knew he had her when she started rocking her hips to the beat of his tongue. She was so wet her pussy juices were rolling down the front of his neck. He pulled out his finishing move on her by bending her leg back the one he had in the crook of his neck and he begin alternating, licking her from her asshole and her pussy. After he had done that about five times each he applied pressure to her clit with his nose and continued licking her tunnel until she came in his mouth.

While he was sucking up all of her juices, she started grinding harder on his face she started mumbling something. Adam couldn't make out what she was saying and he really didn't care. At that time her pussy walls was gripping his tongue as he dug his tongue inside her as deep as he could get it, it was like he was digging for gold. She said it again but this time he heard her, "Ohh Termaine." She said loud and clear. Termaine what the fuck? Who the hell is Termaine? This bitch done lost her mind! Adam thought as he stopped in his tracks out of all the years he had been fucking, hustling, and pimping these hoes he had never been called another niggas name and he wasn't going to start tonight.

Adam stood up letting her leg hit the ground hard and she opened her eyes, "Who the fuck is Termaine?" He asked her with her pussy juices still around his mouth and anger in his voice like he was her man or something.

"Not you nigga!" Diamond said with a smile on her face as she raised her gun up in the air and pointed it at his chest. She saw the look of horror on his face before she emptied her clip in him. Adam grabbed his chest before he fell backwards from the impact of the bullets hitting him.

You see Adam thought Diamond was sleep but she had woke up half way through his oral sex session. When she realized what he was doing and peeped at him out the corners of her eye. This fool was eating her pussy with his eyes closed, she eased one of her hands inside her purse under the cover while the other one guided his face to her pussy. Diamond thought, hell Jay is in jail and Tee Tee was

Diary of a Triflin' Bitch

in a coma I need this nut. This baby got me horny as hell so why not get a good nut on the house.

After she got what she was waiting on out of him she put a quick plan in motion, so she called him another niggas name to piss him off. It worked like a charm. That's what he gets from trying to blackmail a real bitch!

Diamond gathered all of her belongings, wiped down everything she had touched to make sure she didn't leave any of her fingerprints anywhere in the house, and then grabbed her food and left Adam's house. Diamond made it home in no time she ate her food and then she started to clean up her house. She wanted to pack everything up so she could move it into her new apartment she was planning to share with Tee Tee.

Diamond had all the rooms cleaned and cleared out except the guest bedroom. She really didn't want to go in there. She didn't have any of her things in there; it was Brandy's room she slept in when she would stay the night. But if she really wanted to sell this house for a profit she knew she had to clean up every room. She was almost

Diary of a Triflin' Bitch

done cleaning up the room until she opened the nightstand drawer...

What the hell is this? Looks like my diary. Now why in the hell is it in here? Was Brandy reading my shit on the low? Wait a minute this is not mines it's hers. Let me see what this bitch been up to. Diamond said to herself. She finished cleaning the room up, and went to take a shower she was beat from today's events.

Once Diamond got settled from her shower she jumped right into Brandy's diary...

Diary of a Triflin' Bitch

1/14/13

Hey Diary,

Ant came and picked me up from Diamond's house after Tip's party. I had to get the fuck away from her if she ever found out what I did she would kill me. I hate fucking Ant's lil dick ass. We have been fucking since we were in high school. I know the nigga act like he is in love but I'm not. I'm just in love with his money. If he isn't going to become a boss soon then I'm going to leave his ass alone. And I'm going to stop giving him the names of these niggas we be setting up to be robbed. We suppose to hit Kash next week wish me luck. Goodnight.

"Wait a minute, I knew she was fucking Ant but they were setting niggas up to be robbed now that I didn't know. And that's where she disappeared to that night after Tip's party. Wow you never know a person until you get in their head." Diamond kept reading this shit was getting good.

Diary of a Triflin' Bitch

1/20/13

Hey Diary,

I'm so pissed off right now I think I played myself tonight, I was hanging out with some friends when Tee Tee called saying Ant wanted to see me so I went over there. When I got there Ant wasn't there yet so I waited for him. I got bored so I came on to Tee Tee but he wouldn't bite. The nigga wouldn't fuck me but he didn't mind letting me suck his dick. I thought maybe after I put my head game down on his ass he would bend me over and fuck the shit out of me, but he refused to. He made me suck his dick twice and after he came in my face he put me out of the house. WTF was that all about and Ant's ass never called me either. Fuck both of them. Goodnight.

That's what her ass gets always trying to fuck somebody's man. I knew Tee Tee had better sense than to stick his dick in her. But we got to have a talk about this when he gets his ass out the hospital. Diamond flipped a couple of pages until she got to the page where she saw Dayshawn's name.

Diary of a Triflin' Bitch

1/28/13

Hey Diary,

Tonight I went to the trap house to see if I could find Ant or either Tee Tee ass. One of them niggas was going to take me home with them tonight. So I waited until everybody was gone but Dayshawn. Me and him talked and played strip poker for shots of vodka. I won most of the games but Dayshawn got wasted and started coming on to me so me being the triflin' bitch I am. I fucked the shit out of my cousins man. That niggas dick wasn't any good but his tongue was the boom! I fucked the hell out of his face. I never had a man to suck on my clit the way he did I knew he wanted to be my man. Fuck Tracy! Her man is now mines. Goodnight.

"What the fuck!" Was all Diamond could say. "Brandy was fucking Tracy's man up under our noses and none of us knew it. This bitch was very messy if she would fuck her cousin man she would fuck anybody. Even though Diamond was getting madder by the page she flipped the diary to August and got the shock of her life…

Diary of a Triflin' Bitch

2/12/13

Hey Diary,

Tonight I fucked Jay in Diamond's house on her couch while she was at work. That nigga banged my back out. Boy it was so good I knew he didn't love that bitch the way she was putting on. But his dick was a perfect fit and I think I'm in love with my best friend's man. Little do she know it her man is going to be my baby daddy! Goodnight.

"I'm going to kill this bitch and when Jay's ass gets out of jail I'm going to fuck him up to. Now it's on I got to find this bitch Brandy…"

Coming Soon: Diary of a Triflin' Bitch 2……

About The Author

Platinum was born and raised in Bradenton, Florida. She is a new author who reached #1 on Amazon's bestsellers list with this book in the Urban Fiction category. She decided to start writing fiction while on bed rest with her last child. She is currently employed at Quest Diagnostic and she attended Meridian College where she majored in Nursing. Platinum wants to continue her journey in nursing and wants to become an advanced practice registered nurse (APRN). Platinum has four kids and a godson whom she is very proud of. She is currently hard at work on her next book.

Follow Platinum at:
Facebook: facebook.com/youngauthorplatinum
Instagram: @youngauthorplatinum
Twitter: @Author_platinum

Follow Right Circle Publications at:
Facebook: facebook.com/rightcirclepub
Instagram: @rightcirclepub
Twitter: @rigthcirclepub

Made in the USA
Columbia, SC
16 June 2017